Suddenly,

Just for a split second, four familiar figures shoved Bailey toward the back. They were trying to kidnap her! God only knew what they would do if they managed to get her out of there, but he wasn't going to let that happen. He had to stop it.

He rose to his feet and took a deep breath.

Now or never.

If they got her into that van, it was over, and he wasn't going to let the woman he loved be lost to him a second time.

Without another thought, he went sprinting toward them, blazing with all the anger of a bat out of hell and ready to put these guys down.

For good.

PROTECTIVE LAWMAN

JANIE CROUCH

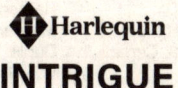

INTRIGUE

If you purchased this book without a cover you should be aware that this book is stolen property. It was reported as "unsold and destroyed" to the publisher, and neither the author nor the publisher has received any payment for this "stripped book."

This book is dedicated to the little girl who came up to me at a restaurant and told me I was "so pretty"… Kid, you have no idea how your sweet words made my heart sing. May we all remember to be so kind.

Recycling programs for this product may not exist in your area.

ISBN-13: 978-1-335-69037-1

Protective Lawman

Copyright © 2025 by Janie Crouch

All rights reserved. No part of this book may be used or reproduced in any manner whatsoever without written permission.

Without limiting the exclusive rights of any author, contributor or the publisher of this publication, any unauthorized use of this publication to train generative artificial intelligence (AI) technologies is expressly prohibited. Harlequin also exercises their rights under Article 4(3) of the Digital Single Market Directive 2019/790 and expressly reserves this publication from the text and data mining exception.

This is a work of fiction. Names, characters, places and incidents are either the product of the author's imagination or are used fictitiously. Any resemblance to actual persons, living or dead, businesses, companies, events or locales is entirely coincidental.

For questions and comments about the quality of this book, please contact us at CustomerService@Harlequin.com.

TM and ® are trademarks of Harlequin Enterprises ULC.

 Harlequin Enterprises ULC
22 Adelaide St. West, 41st Floor
Toronto, Ontario M5H 4E3, Canada
www.Harlequin.com

HarperCollins Publishers
Macken House, 39/40 Mayor Street Upper,
Dublin 1, D01 C9W8, Ireland
www.HarperCollins.com

Printed in Lithuania

Janie Crouch writes passionate romantic suspense for readers who still believe in heroes. After a lifetime on the East Coast—and a six-year stint in Germany—this *USA TODAY* bestselling author has settled into her dream home in the Front Range of the Colorado Rockies. She loves engaging in all sorts of adventures (triathlons! two-hundred-mile relay races! mountain treks!), traveling and surviving life with four kids. You can find out more about her at janiecrouch.com.

Books by Janie Crouch

Harlequin Intrigue

Warrior Peak Sanctuary

Protective Assignment
Protective Lawman

San Antonio Security

Texas Bodyguard: Luke
Texas Bodyguard: Brax
Texas Bodyguard: Weston
Texas Bodyguard: Chance

The Risk Series: A Bree and Tanner Thriller

Calculated Risk
Security Risk
Constant Risk
Risk Everything

Omega Sector: Under Siege

Daddy Defender
Protector's Instinct
Cease Fire

Visit the Author Profile page
at Harlequin.com for more titles.

CAST OF CHARACTERS

Aaron Ward—Former police officer who discovered corruption in his department and nearly lost everything because of it. Now works at the Warrior Peak Sanctuary.

Bailey Masters—Aaron's young partner when he was an officer; didn't understand how he could up and leave her the way he did.

Cade Thatcher—Former soldier who now works at the Warrior Peak Sanctuary and leads tactical missions there. Engaged to River.

River Robertson—Works at the Warrior Peak Sanctuary as an assistant to the counselor. Engaged to Cade.

Xavier Michaels—Former CIA agent and co-owner of Warrior Peak Sanctuary, runs the day-to-day operations of the center.

Lawson Davies—Former Army Special Forces and co-owner of Warrior Peak Sanctuary. He runs their tactical unit.

Hannah Davies—Lawson's younger sister who works at Warrior Peak Sanctuary. Always ready to help with a friendly smile.

Prologue

Officer Aaron Ward sighed in frustration as he closed another case file. He rubbed his eyes, which were gritty with exhaustion, and decided he was going to need another cup of coffee—or seven.

For a few months he had suspected that something not quite aboveboard was going on in North Carolina's Kings Mountain Police Department, where he worked. He had started poking around as inconspicuously as he could. Paying attention to what certain officers were—or weren't—doing, and taking a closer look at the ones he thought might be involved in suspicious activities.

Of course, he couldn't do this during normal work hours because he had his actual job to do, plus he didn't want anyone to know what he was doing yet. So, he'd been putting in extra hours, staying at the station long into the night when he should have been home sleeping. Hence the need for more coffee.

He knew he would need to take this up the chain of command eventually, but he wanted to gather more concrete evidence first. He couldn't request a meeting with his captain or the chief of police and only present his own opinions and suspicions. He had sworn an oath to serve and protect the community of Kings Mountain, and he intended to do that, even from other officers who didn't take that oath as seriously as he did.

He was getting close to gathering enough evidence. There was a group of officers that he suspected were corrupt—taking bribes, withholding important investigative information, and bullying witnesses, among a laundry list of other shady things. He needed to make sure that he knew which officers were involved and in what capacity.

He saved the most recent case file he'd looked at to a folder on his computer and decided to call it a night. He'd have to be back at the station in just a few hours, and he was going to need some rest if he was going to be able to work a full day and then put in more hours afterward again. Plus, he got to work with Bailey tomorrow. She was new to the force but she was a good officer and he enjoyed working with her. There were other feelings there too that he refused to acknowledge, especially while he was her superior.

He powered down his computer, turned off the lamp on his desk, and walked toward the parking lot, his mind still running through the information he'd found. He was about halfway across the lot when he heard the sound of another car door shutting. He didn't think much of it; it was a police station, after all, and people were around at all hours of the day and night. But when he looked in the direction of the sound, he saw that there were several men approaching him quickly.

Warning bells went off in his mind. This wasn't normal. He continued walking to his car, hoping that if he didn't engage them, they would continue on without bothering him.

No such luck.

He squinted as the men got closer, trying to make out who they were.

"Hello, Ward," one of them sneered.

Ziegler.

"Hey, guys. What brings you here at this hour?" Aaron asked.

Ziegler laughed humorlessly. "We could ask you the same thing."

Aaron shrugged. "Just finishing up some work."

Ziegler moved closer, getting in Aaron's face and pinning him against his car. His cronies—Moore, Benning, and Lee—flanked him. "Yeah, that's why we're here, snitch."

Aaron's stomach dropped. So he'd been right. These guys were crooked.

"We know you've been keeping tabs on us and doing your own little investigation." Ziegler poked a finger hard into Aaron's chest. "You're not as sneaky as you think you are."

Ziegler pulled his arm back and slammed it into Aaron's gut. He doubled over in pain, gasping for air. "And just so you know," Ziegler spat, "we have eyes on your precious Bailey right now. She's at home, reading a book. And we could take her out in a second if you don't get out of town, and pretend none of this ever happened. You understand?"

Before he could reply, Moore jerked Aaron upright and Ziegler hit him again, this time in the jaw, knocking him to the ground. All bets were off as soon as he went down. Before Aaron could attempt to regain his footing, Benning started kicking him in the chest while Moore jammed his boot repeatedly in his back.

Aaron tried to fight back, but once the other men joined in, he knew there was no way he could win. Ziegler, not to be left out of their fun, focused on his face and head. The more they beat him, the more he wondered if he'd even survive. Pain was radiating throughout his entire body and he was pretty sure they broke some ribs, among other things. His last thought before everything went black was that he had to get Bailey away from these men, before she got hurt too.

Chapter One

Six Years Later

Bailey Masters smiled to herself as she rounded the corner, and the small town of Kings Mountain came into view. Finally. After all this time, she was back home again.

It felt like a lifetime since she had left Kings Mountain and, in some ways, it had been. Her life here had been so different from the one she'd led before, sometimes it was hard to remember that she had lived here, worked here, and made a name for herself here when she had been a rookie cop.

She could still remember the first day she stepped into the station, that flood of pride and excitement that hit her like a ton of bricks. She had wanted to be a cop for as long as she could remember, arresting her toys and reading them their rights before she put them in a little makeshift prison made from her toy box when she was a kid. It had always been in her blood, and she had been determined to make it as soon as she found out it was a career option for her.

But that had been before—before she'd been kicked out and moved across the country, before she had faced up to the fact that the man she had idolized—and almost loved, too—had turned his back on her and made it clear what he really thought of her.

Sometimes, she struggled even thinking about him. She grimaced as she drove down into the town, through the familiar streets she had called home for so long. How long had it been? Six years? Just over that now. There had been a time when she was sure she would never get back, but the relief of finally having returned to her hometown wasn't going to be ruined by the memories of the man who had thrown her out of it in the first place.

Aaron.

She tried not to think about him. The two of them had been assigned to work together when she had first been starting out, and she had been so excited. Working with someone like him, someone with his reputation and impressive backlist of cases, she knew she was going to learn so much.

And she did. Because the two of them worked together really well. Or, at least, that was what she'd thought, before reality had slapped her in the face. They would spend most of every day together, driving around and helping out with whatever small cases the people around the town needed them to look at. They got to know each other really well, because how could you not in those circumstances? They understood each other better than anyone else in the world. Even now, knowing what he had done, she still missed him.

She had developed a crush on him, of course. All the time they spent together, combined with his charming personality, made it impossible not to fall for him. At least a little bit. She told herself it would fade with time, but if anything, it had just grown more insistent. She couldn't deny how she felt about him, and she didn't want to. No, she wanted to spend even more time with him, get to know him even more deeply than she had. She could tell from the way he looked at her sometimes that the thought had at least crossed his mind, too.

And then he'd betrayed her. Written a scornful report that had landed her being stuck at a desk job across the country for years now. She still didn't know exactly what he'd put in there, but it had been enough to get her blackballed from her old position and moved into a new one she would never in a million years have asked for. Almost in the blink of an eye, too.

The added kicker of it was, he hadn't even had the guts to face her and do it himself. He'd just turned in the report and called out of work—faking sick—and had someone else do his dirty work. She'd even had a weak moment after the shock of it wore off and tried to contact him, with no response. Not that she had been surprised by then.

Sometimes, she still had a hard time believing it. She had turned it over a thousand times in her head, trying to figure out what had caused him to turn on her the way he had, but she had never been able to figure it out. Either way, that wasn't the problem now. He was out of her life, and she wanted it to stay that way. Anyone who would stab her in the back the way he had wasn't the kind of person she wanted in her life.

She focused her gaze on the road ahead, and took the turn at the end of Main Street to take her to the police station. It was going to be so weird, being around all the people she had started out with when she was a rookie cop. She had been so young when she'd first begun her tenure here, just out of training and ready to take on the world. She could still remember the excitement she had felt, how much she had looked forward to every day at work. Her other friends from high school were in college or had started to settle down and raise families, but her career was the only thing she gave a damn about.

She pulled the truck to a halt outside the station, and paused for a moment before she turned off the engine and got out. How would she be greeted? Would they be friendly or skeptical of her being back after all these years? What were they going to say when they saw her again? Of course, they knew she was coming, but seeing her in person was going to be different.

What if they thought she had gone soft from being behind a desk for so long? She hoped they knew that she'd been struggling the whole time, wishing she could get back out in the field as she filed endless stacks of paperwork. She had fantasized all day long about getting back out there, about actually making a difference and helping people in the real world again. There might have been cops who were happy behind a desk doing paperwork, and that was fine for them, but that was not her. She wanted more.

She always had.

She climbed out of her truck, strode toward the door, and mustered up all her courage. She wasn't actually starting work until the next day, but she wanted to check in and see what was happening right now and say hello to whoever was inside. She was looking forward to seeing the people she used to work with again.

She had been invited back to a couple of events around

the holidays the first year after she left, but honestly, she couldn't stand the thought of facing them after the embarrassment of being ousted and forced to ride a desk instead of being out in the field doing real cop work. She knew she was better than that, and she hated even the idea of being seen as some pencil pusher locked away in an office all day long instead of on the streets, working cases and helping others. Living her dream.

But now? It was different. She was back on the beat again. Back out and ready to take on the world. She could hardly wait to see what it had to offer. Pushing open the door, she stepped inside, and was greeted by a round of hellos from the cops she had worked with as a younger woman.

"Wow, Bailey, I can't believe you actually made it," Philip Benning exclaimed, jumping up from his desk and hurrying over to her. "Thought you would have been safer behind that desk in Pallas Bay."

"Safer, but way more bored," Bailey replied with a chuckle, and she reached to give him a hug. She normally wasn't a hugger, but seeing these guys again after so long had her feeling sentimental.

Brian Lee, one of the older cops who served as the muscle for the station, emerged from his office and grinned when he saw Bailey standing there.

"You made it back," he said.

She nodded. "Took me long enough."

A moment later, Stanley Moore and Jay Ziegler appeared from their offices and came over to greet her, too.

"Good to have you back," Ziegler told her.

She grinned widely. She couldn't keep the smile off her face. She was back—she was really, truly, finally back.

"Yeah, good to be here," she replied. "So, what needs to be done? What cases are you working right now?"

Ziegler laughed. "You've only just arrived," he reminded her. "Take a minute to catch your breath before you dive back into work."

"I've been stuck at a desk for years," she shot back. "I've waited long enough."

"We're actually just finishing up for the day," Lee said. "We were going to head down to the bar. You want to come with? Catch up before you're back on tomorrow."

"That sounds great," she agreed.

She had been on the road all day, and the thought of a cold beer was tempting.

The guys packed up and headed out to their cars and down the street to the bar. Bailey followed in her truck, glancing around as she took in the familiar sights around her. It was going to be a while before she really felt settled here again, but just being back was everything she had been dreaming of these last few years.

Well, almost everything. Maybe it wouldn't be the same without Aaron. Working with him had been one of the things she loved most about the job. She knew things were going to be different than when she'd worked in Kings Mountain before.

But it was better this way.

She never wanted to see him again as long as she lived. He must hate her. Nobody could betray someone like he'd betrayed her and not hate their guts. She didn't need that kind of negativity in her life. She was back in Kings Mountain and nothing—and no one—was going to mess it up for her this time. She'd worked too hard to get to where she was to let someone from her past affect her present or future.

When she got to the bar, she noticed the guys were already inside. She must have been a little more lost in her head than she thought, so she quickly jumped out of her truck and hurried to join them. They were just walking up to the bar, so Bailey rushed forward to buy the first round of drinks. She was determined to make a good impression so they'd see her as a team player from the start and want to keep her around. They retreated to a table at the back of the room, and she noticed a few people glancing in their direction. Some of them were familiar faces—cops she hadn't seen in years—and some were regular patrons winding down after work or meeting up with friends.

"To Bailey's return!" Ziegler led a toast, and everyone clinked their beers together. Bailey sipped on hers, not wanting to get carried away, and her eyes darted around the table. She had been out with these guys before, but there had always been someone else there, too. Someone she couldn't help but miss, despite all of her better judgment.

"So, what have you guys been up to these days?" Bailey inquired, hoping to get a little background of what'd been happening lately.

"Ah, same old, same old. Not much has changed. We're still kicking ass and taking names," Ziegler replied with a dark chuckle. Her eyes darted to him, and she started to feel a little uneasy at his tone.

"Still the biggest and baddest," Moore added with a smirk.

"Here, here!" they all called out, and clinked their bottles together again.

"Where's Aaron these days?" she asked, doing her best to keep her voice casual. She figured it was better to just ask upfront. No point in pretending she didn't notice his absence.

"Oh, I heard he's fixing fences for some lodge for wimps, even if they call it Warrior Peak," Lee replied, waving his hand. "Haven't heard from him since...well, since you left, actually."

"Good riddance," Benning muttered, shaking his head. Her ears perked up at once.

"What do you mean?"

"We're better off without him," Lee cut in, trying to shut down Benning before he said too much.

"Yeah, we don't need his whistleblowing ass," Benning snapped.

Bailey froze for a moment, not sure how to respond.

"Whistleblowing?" she asked, the hairs on the back of her neck standing on end.

"Yeah, we don't need someone who doesn't stand by his fellow cops," Ziegler added. Suddenly, the atmosphere at the table changed and she felt the tension rise. Something was off, and she didn't like it at all.

"But that's not a problem we're going to have with you, is it?" he asked, leaning toward Bailey.

She drew her beer closer to her, as though it might provide some degree of protection.

What were they talking about? Aaron was a whistleblower? When had this happened? Or...or was that why she had been sent away? Her mind raced, but she could tell one thing for sure—this wasn't the welcoming outing she had thought it was.

Ziegler lowered his voice, making sure only Bailey could hear him.

"Exactly how far are you willing to go to keep this job, Bailey?" he asked her.

She shifted in her seat. *Crap.* She had no idea what to say.

Instead of answering him, she pasted on a smile and stood up. "Well, guys, it was great to hang out like old times but I better be going. I still have a lot of unpacking to do at my new place, and I want to be rested for my first day back on the beat tomorrow."

She tossed a few bills on the table to cover her half-finished beer and turned to leave, trying to look casual as she walked away and not like she was rushing toward the exit. Her heart was pounding in her chest as she headed to the door and she could feel their eyes on her. It took all her willpower not to glance over her shoulder.

She waved to a few people she recognized on her way out but once she was outside, she started walking faster. The bar was crowded so her truck was parked pretty far back in the lot. She was about halfway across the lot when the loud music from inside the bar filtered out like someone had opened the door.

Deep down she knew it was them and real panic was setting in fast, but she still didn't look back. She kept herself moving as quickly as she dared toward the safety of her truck. She allowed herself to feel a little bit of relief as the truck finally came into view.

Had she blown that conversation in the bar out of proportion? It had made her uncomfortable, but the guys hadn't said or done anything explicitly damning. Maybe she had overreacted.

She would have to apologize for her quick and awkward exit tomorrow at work. But just as that thought entered her mind, she heard a noise close behind her. She spun around to see Ziegler and the others closing in.

"Where are you going in such a hurry, Bailey?" Benning said in a taunting voice.

"Like I said, I need to unpack and get some rest," she said, trying to keep her voice steady.

Just another few steps and she'd be at her truck. She kept the men in view but continued backing toward the driver's door. They were in a dark corner in the back of the parking lot where no one would hear her call for help. And even if she'd parked closer to the bar, the music was so loud that it was unlikely that anyone would hear her. She was going to have to do this alone.

"Stop right there, Bailey. We just want to talk," Ziegler said.

Her back hit the side of her truck. She realized too late that she had made a tactical error by effectively trapping herself between the truck at her back and the men in front. Now there was no way she'd be able to get herself into the safety of her truck without turning her back on her enemy. A rookie mistake. She'd spent too many years behind a desk, after all.

She was out of time. She needed to do something. Fast.

With one final deep breath she swiveled her upper body as quickly as she could to reach for the door handle. But it wasn't enough. She heard someone move and in the next moment she was slammed into the side of her truck with the men crowding her on all sides. She felt hands groping her, someone yanking her head back, hot breath on her neck, and then someone smashed her head into the side of the truck. The hit was hard enough to stun her, and caused her to groan in pain.

She could hear the men murmuring at her back and everything started to spin as she was quickly whipped around to face them. Spots danced before her eyes and a flash of something shiny—a knife? —was coming toward her. It was the last thing she saw before everything went black.

BAILEY SLOWLY REGAINED CONSCIOUSNESS, moaning at the pain racking her entire body. Her head was pounding and she could tell her leg was bleeding, but beyond that, she had no clue what the damage was. Just that everything hurt.

One thing she did know—she needed to get off the ground and get out of that parking lot immediately.

She got herself into a sitting position, trying to clear the cobwebs from her head. She looked around, taking in her surroundings as best she could. Cars were still in the parking lot and music was still blaring from the bar. She must not have been out for too long. She didn't sense anyone nearby, but she still felt an urgency pushing her into action.

Leaning heavily on her truck, she pulled herself up to standing and gripped the side panel when everything started to sway. Concussion? Probably. Blood loss...definitely. She untucked her shirt and ripped the hem so she could make a tourniquet for her leg. She'd figure out the rest of her injuries later but she needed to stop the bleeding now.

Once she had her leg wrapped, she worked her way to the driver's door and slid into the seat. She had no idea what had just happened, or why. But she knew one person who would be able to shed a little light on this whole situation. The one person she had sworn she would avoid as long as possible.

Aaron.

Chapter Two

Aaron hissed with pain as he felt a sliver slide into his palm. He really should have been used to it by now, but the splinters always got him. That's what he got for not wearing gloves. Leaning down, he drew his hand into his mouth and sucked until he felt the splinter dislodge, and spat it to the ground before he stood back to admire his handiwork.

See, now *this* had been worth a few splinters. For the last few months, he had been working on rebuilding the outbuildings for the horses here at the Warrior Peak Sanctuary. He was fixing them up so they could keep the hay dry during the spring, and so the horses would have somewhere to shelter out of the heat of the sun. It would be summer soon and he didn't want to leave them with nowhere to rest on a hot day.

And he had done a pretty good job of it, if he said so himself. It had been almost relaxing for him, being able to come out here every day and enjoy the peace and quiet as he set to work with his hands. As the end of spring approached, it seemed like the whole landscape was blooming to life around them, green punctuated by purples and reds as flowers began to blossom. Against the clear blue sky above, it was downright gorgeous. Another reminder as to why he had come here—and why he had been so willing to leave his old life behind to do so.

He was about to get back to work when he heard a whistle from behind him, and he turned to see Lawson Davies, one of the owners of the lodge, striding toward him through the long grass.

"Hey," Aaron called to him.

Something shifted as Lawson got closer to him, a tingling in his palms—it was something he'd learned back in the day that meant he should be worried. He tried to push that aside, reminding himself he was safe here. At least, that was what he hoped.

"Hi," Lawson replied as he glanced over to the work Aaron had been doing. "It's looking pretty good out here."

"Just 'pretty good'?" Aaron shot back.

Lawson grinned. "Hey, I actually came here for a reason," he remarked. "There's someone up at the main lodge asking for you."

A ripple of uneasiness pulsed through Aaron's body. "Who is it?"

"I don't know," Lawson replied with a shrug. "But they came asking for you specifically. Seemed pretty important."

Who the hell could have found Aaron out here? The whole point of coming to this place was that it was in the middle of nowhere. Nobody should have been able to find him out here. His eyes darted back and forth, looking around as though the answer to his question might have been somewhere in the forest surrounding the field.

"Should I be concerned that there are strangers asking for my handyman?" Lawson asked, clocking Aaron's body language.

Aaron tried to relax and shook his head quickly. The last thing he wanted was for any of them to second-guess his presence here. This place was the best thing that could have happened to him in the aftermath of his life imploding, and he wasn't going to let anything get in the way of it.

"It's a woman, if that changes anything," Lawson offered. "Pretty, red hair, green eyes. She didn't give a name and it looks like she's been through it."

"'Been through it'? What does that mean?" Aaron asked.

"She drove up in a beat-up truck and looks a little rough herself," Lawson replied. "But you should come see for yourself. She seemed pretty insistent. Said she'd only talk to you."

"Yeah. Sure," Aaron replied, tossing down his tools to follow Lawson back to the main building. His mind raced as he tried to put the pieces together.

Who could possibly be looking for him here? He had come here to get away from everything that had happened before, and he wasn't sure what he would do if his past came back to haunt him after all this time. There was a nudge in the back of his mind but he refused to let it surface. He'd known a beautiful redhead with bright green eyes and a sassy attitude years ago. But there was no way she would be there looking for him.

As he walked, his mind rushed through other potential people it might be. He didn't have family, no sisters, aunts, or cousins who might have come looking for him. So who the hell was this? And how did she find him?

"There, that's her truck," Lawson told him, pointing to a beat-up blue truck sitting in the main parking area. Aaron stared at it for a moment, willing it to bring back some memories that would help him make sense of all of this, but he was coming up blank.

"Ring any bells?" Lawson asked curiously.

He shook his head. "Guess I need to see her," Aaron replied, trying to keep his voice steady.

He could count on one hand the number of times people had come to Warrior Peak looking for him over the last six years. He tried to convince himself that it was nothing to worry about, even if his mind was running so fast he was having a hard time getting his thoughts under control. He didn't want his fear to show on his face.

Lawson had been kind enough not to demand too much in the way of explanation when it came to his presence here. Neither he nor the others pushed him to share his past and what brought him to the lodge all those years ago. They knew there was something Aaron was running from. Hell, he'd arrived broken and bruised and paranoid of almost everything. So it wasn't a huge leap to think he'd suffered some sort of trauma. But they never pushed. Just offered support and assistance for him to get back on his feet and then offered him a job, if he wanted to stay. So, he did. He'd given up everything from his old life and made a new start here at Warrior Peak. He'd burned the only connection he'd ever cared about and didn't have anything to go back to, anyway.

Inside, the main building was quiet except for a few people chatting in the corridor as Lawson led Aaron down to the meeting rooms. Who was there for him? His mind drifted back to the truck. Something about it had twinged something in his gut, and he wasn't sure what it was.

Maybe he should just turn around and tell Lawson that he had changed his mind. He'd rather head back out to continue his work, anyway. He couldn't think of any good reasons why a random woman would be here looking for him. It could only mean trouble.

But when he saw Xavier Michaels, Lawson's business partner, pacing in the small space outside the meeting rooms, he knew he wasn't going to be let off that easily.

Xavier raised his eyebrows at him. "What's going on here, Ward?" When he used his last name, Aaron knew Xavier was not happy with him. He wasn't sure exactly why he was mad at him, but he'd do whatever was necessary to make it right. This place had been a sanctuary for Aaron since he had left his old life, and he would do anything it took to make sure that didn't change.

"What has she said to you?" Aaron asked, trying to keep his voice even. He didn't want Xavier to think he was worried. Xavier was protective of Warrior Peak, of everything they had managed to do here, and he wasn't going to let anything get in the way of it.

"Nothing," came Xavier's frustrated reply. "She's said she's only willing to talk to you. Wouldn't even give us a name."

Aaron sighed.

"And she won't let anyone treat her injuries. At least until she sees you," he added.

Aaron froze. Injuries? Why was an injured woman here looking for him? This was bad news. Really, really bad. The nudge in the back of his mind was getting more insistent.

"I'll talk to her," Aaron replied, rolling back his shoulders. Whatever he had to handle here, he could take it on.

"She's got an attitude on her," Xavier warned him. "I don't know what she just walked out of, but her fuse is basically nonexistent."

"I can handle that," Aaron replied. He'd been a cop, after all. He knew how to handle people in high-pressure situations, and he wasn't going to let his fear get the better of him.

Xavier jerked his head toward the door, and Lawson stepped over to it. The glass was frosted, blocking out his view of whoever was inside, but he could make out the dark shape of someone sitting there. Someone waiting for him.

Someone who might just know who he really was.

Xavier pushed the door open. "Miss. Aaron is here to see you."

"He is?"

Aaron's body tensed when he heard that voice. He had never imagined in a million years that he would ever get a chance to hear it again. His heart leaped into his throat as he pushed by Xavier and stepped inside the room.

There, wincing as she propped herself up on the chair opposite him, was the green-eyed, redheaded ghost from his past.

Bailey.

Chapter Three

Bailey gripped her stomach as she tried to stand up to greet him, but the throbbing in her thigh and various aches and pains overloading her body caused her to rethink that idea so she settled back in the chair. He pushed the door shut behind him, giving them some privacy.

Bailey stared up at him. Aaron. Aaron Ward. She couldn't believe it. He turned back to face her, and looked down at her for a moment. His eyes roamed her form, stopping on each injury, causing her to shift in her seat under his intense gaze.

Her heart twisted in her chest. It was him. It was really, truly him.

"Bailey?" he murmured. God, it had been so long since she'd heard him say her name, and something in her softened at once. All of the memories of them were flooding back to her, all the safety and comfort she'd felt in his presence. It was exactly why she'd come here. She knew there was nobody she could trust like him, even after what he'd done to her.

And, after what had happened last night, she knew she needed him more than ever.

He moved through the room, pulling the curtains shut, and she followed him with her eyes. He looked just the same as ever—the same purposeful gait, the same piercing green eyes, the same broad shoulders. She was even sure he was wearing the same aftershave, the scent drifting through the air as he walked by her. Mixed with something else, too—wood, the smell of grass.

But there were a few differences that she noticed as she kept watching him. Out of his police uniform, in a pair of jeans and a casual shirt, he looked more...relaxed. His light brown hair was a little grown out, and there was a smattering of stubble on his chin.

The same man who had betrayed her all those years ago. But the only person she could think of to run to when things had gone bad. Her mind ran in a million different directions. There was so much she wanted to say to him and ask him, but she also wanted to chew him the hell out for what he had done to her. She had sworn to herself she would never see him again, but here she was, sitting in front of him, and praying he was going to be able to help her.

"Are you okay?" Aaron asked as he noticed her wincing again.

She pressed her hand into her lower rib cage, trying to stem the bolt of pain that was rushing up her side. "I'm fine."

"You don't look fine," Aaron replied skeptically.

She shook her head. "It's not as bad as it looks."

"You've had someone take a look at you?"

"Not yet," she admitted. She hadn't had time to stop by a hospital to get checked out, and she could feel the wetness of the blood starting to seep from her leg again. She thought she had stopped the bleeding, but clearly, that wasn't the case.

"You need to let someone here take a look," he told her.

She shook her head. She didn't want to be seen by anyone else if she could help it. What if some of the people here were working with *them*? What was going to happen to her? If they found her, they might not let her walk away this time.

"I'm fine," she attempted to say again, but her voice wavered dangerously as the blood began to leak through her jeans once more.

"You're bleeding," Aaron replied bluntly.

"Nothing I can't handle," she replied.

"Then why are you here?"

Bailey felt her cheeks heat. He had called her bluff, and he was right. She wouldn't have come here, to him of all people, if she thought there was any chance in hell that she could handle the situation herself. He stepped back, giving her the space she needed, but she could see the concern written all over his face.

"Because I got into some trouble and I need a place to lie low until I can get back on my feet," she replied.

Did he buy it? She scanned his expression, trying to read what was going on in his mind. She used to know him so well, she could tell what he was thinking just from a look—but it had been so long now she wasn't sure what the furrow in his brow meant.

That was all she was going to give him, for now. She needed to rest and clear her head before she got into details. She couldn't risk spilling the truth of what had happened to drive her out here before she was ready. She had no idea how she had even managed to find this place, but when she had staggered in to the reception and told them she was here for Aaron, she knew at once that she had come to the right place. The shock on the face of the woman behind the desk as she'd darted off to find someone else was burned into her brain. Did she really look that rough?

"So, why did you ask specifically for me? If you were just coming here to lie low, there was no reason for me to even know you were here."

Damn. He had a point. He would be the last person she would want to see, so what made her ask for him? What would he believe?

"I heard you might be here, so I asked. I really wasn't expecting you to show up after—" She snapped her lips closed. She didn't want to open that can of worms right now. She had enough on her plate to deal with. "It doesn't matter. Call it curiosity, that's all."

He narrowed his eyes at her, weighing her words. She knew he didn't believe her, but hopefully he wouldn't call her on it now.

"Fine," Aaron replied, shaking his head. "What can we do to help?"

He hadn't changed. Always focusing on the practical solutions to any problem and what he could do to make the situation better. That was Aaron in a nutshell. She wasn't sure she needed anything practical right now, though. She wasn't even sure how to feel about all of this.

She was scared and worried they were going to find her and finish what they started last night. She was still sad and angry about Aaron's betrayal, but she also felt unexpected joy and another feeling she couldn't quite name now that he was standing in front of her. It was all just too much right now to process.

Bailey slowly released the breath she didn't realize

she was holding, then winced at the movement. She really needed to get someone to look at her injuries. She was starting to feel a little woozy.

"It's fine, I'll figure it out. Sorry to pull you away from whatever you were doing. You can go," she replied, though she hoped he wouldn't take her up on that. Even though she was still mad and confused, she wanted him here with her. She was scared. Really, really scared. She had never been hurt this badly. Her whole body was in pain. She'd been running on pure adrenaline until she had gotten here, but now that she could actually rest, she felt like she might pass out.

"You can't dismiss me. I'm not going to leave you to figure things out alone, Bailey," he replied firmly. He crouched down in front of her. Even as her vision started to get a little hazy, she could make out the piercing green of his eyes.

His eyes swept up and down her body again. She knew she looked horrible, and that she was going to need medical attention if she was going to avoid any long-term issues. But the thought of doing anything except sitting—or lying—down was too exhausting, she couldn't force herself to care.

"Who did this to you?" he asked, his voice low and angry. Like he wanted to take them on himself, make them pay for what they had done to her. She didn't know what to say. Part of her wanted to blurt it all out to him, tell him the truth and beg him to protect her against what was coming her way. Another part of her wanted to run and tell him to forget he had ever seen her again.

Suddenly, it was all too much, emotions and pain both battling for dominance. Emotions seemed to be winning as anger sparked in her chest. She managed to sit herself fully upright, and looked him in the eye.

"You don't get to know that," she growled at him. She knew she was being irrational, but once the anger started rising, she couldn't stop it. He was the one who had turned his back on her and gotten her blacklisted and put on desk duty with whatever he had written in that report. Now he was acting like he cared and wanted to help? She knew she must seem crazy since she was the one who had come to him, but she couldn't stop herself.

"Bailey, I'm trying to help you," he told her, his voice as patient as it could be, given the circumstances. "We have people here who can check you out and make sure you don't need any further treatment. There's a hospital—"

"I don't want to go to hospital," she snarled. She was desperate for him to help her, but seeing him again like this was like a blade through her heart. Her pride was holding her back. She didn't want to have to rely on him, not after what he had done to her.

Planting her hand on the chair for leverage, she dragged herself to her feet. Her knees shook wildly, and her head spun when she was upright. Her body screamed at her to sit back down, but she ignored it. She glared at him, unable to believe she had been foolish enough to come here. Why did she think he, of all people, would be able to help her when he had been the one to wreck her life in the first place? She was such an idiot. A scared and desperate idiot.

She started toward the door as fast as her injured legs would allow. "I shouldn't have come here."

"Bailey, sit down," he ordered her, a hint of the old

cop in him coming through again. He tried to catch her around the waist as she wobbled dangerously, but she pushed him off before he could get hold of her. She didn't want his help.

"This was a mistake," she said, as she continued to inch her way to the door with her hand on the wall to steady herself. She just had to make it back to her truck, then she could rest for a while before getting back on the road to God knows where.

"You're still the same bastard you were when you ruined my life six years ago!" she exclaimed. She whipped her head around to face him when she dropped that bomb. She had no idea if he knew that she was aware he had been the reason she'd ended up in the Bay for so long. Stuck out there behind a desk in the middle of nowhere, wasting her training and potential, when she could be making a difference out on the street.

"What are you talking about—Bailey!" he exclaimed, as she buckled and fell against the door. She managed to catch herself just before her head went crashing into it, and she righted herself too quickly. Dark spots appeared all over her vision, and she knew she was going down.

This time, as she slipped to the ground, Aaron didn't wait. He reached an arm out and caught her, wrapping it around her waist before she could hit the ground. She felt almost weightless as he lifted her into his arms before laying her down on the couch. Her eyes felt so heavy she couldn't keep them open any longer. She could hear voices, though they sounded distant.

"Someone come help!" Aaron called out the door. Her head slumped to the side as the pain and exhaustion pulled her under. All of her fight and anger that was keeping her upright melted away. She couldn't remember why it mattered in the first place.

Her mind sank into the blackness of unconsciousness. The only thing left was the aching pain tearing through every inch of her body.

Chapter Four

Aaron paced back and forth outside the door as he tried to listen in to what was going on inside. He knew he should give River the space to work, but he wasn't going to be able to rest until he knew Bailey was okay.

His mind was racing. He had no idea what she was doing here, and judging by the way she had blown up at him when he had tried to find out, she wasn't going to be forthcoming with the answers. Who had hurt her like that? It killed him to see her so beaten-up, and she wouldn't even tell him who had done it.

But he had an idea. How could he not? It was the same thing that had been hanging over his head for all these years, even though he had tried to leave it behind. Getting her out of there had been the only way he could think of to protect her. He had accepted that she would hate him for what he'd done, but he figured that would make it easier for her to move on. She wouldn't come looking for him, because she wouldn't want anything to do with him.

For the last six years, that seemed to have been true. He hadn't heard from her. And he had accepted that he was never going to see her again, even though the thought of being without her stung. The two of them had worked so well together, but it was more than that. Her sweetness, her sense of humor, her laugh—all of it had led to him developing feelings that were totally not appropriate for someone in his position.

He had tried to ignore it for so long, but even six years later he still dreamed of her sometimes. He missed her so much, he couldn't think about anything else some nights, but he had accepted it was over between them. As if someone like her would ever have been seriously interested in a man like him, anyway. She probably had a million guys who would love to take her on a date. Guys who she didn't have a past with. Hell, she could be involved with someone now. He didn't think that was the case, though. If she was with someone else, why not go to him? Why seek Aaron out instead?

But she had come to him. And he couldn't for the life of him figure out how she knew where he was, or that he would even have been able to help her when she arrived. Some part of her, even if that part was buried so deep down under her anger that she couldn't feel it, knew he would do whatever it took to make sure she stayed safe.

River, Cade's fiancée, was working on her right now. River wasn't a doctor but she had extensive medical training from growing up in a wilderness compound. He prayed she would be able to handle Bailey's injuries. If not, he'd need to drive Bailey in to town to the doctor, or maybe even the hospital, depending on what kind of injuries River found. He didn't know exactly what had happened to her, but from what he could see, she looked bad and he could tell she was in a lot of pain. He had gone so far, done things he could never have imagined, to try and protect her, but what if it hadn't been enough? What if she was still in danger?

Warrior Peak Sanctuary was a place for military and law enforcement members to come and heal when they needed it—physically or mentally. But he'd never dreamed Bailey would be one of those people.

Xavier rounded the corner, followed by Lawson, and Aaron could tell from the looks on their faces that they had some serious questions for him. And he couldn't blame them. This woman had just turned up out of nowhere, after all. This place was important to them, and they weren't going to let anyone in who they didn't totally trust.

"Are you going to tell us what's going on with her?" Lawson demanded, nodding toward the door.

Aaron sighed. He didn't even know where to start. Their relationship had been so damn complicated, and it didn't look like it was about to get easier anytime soon.

"I used to work with her," he explained, trying to keep it vague. "We...she started out as a rookie when I was a cop. I was training her."

"How long ago?"

"A little over six years now," Aaron told Lawson, sinking down into one of the seats outside the room. He could hear River talking to Bailey inside, her tone soothing, though he couldn't make out what she was saying.

Xavier and Lawson exchanged curious looks. "Why would she come and find you after all this time? And what happened between the two of you?" Xavier finally asked.

Aaron stared off into space for a moment as he tried to figure out how best to answer that question. He knew they deserved an answer. They had been kind enough not to press for information about his past when he had first arrived. Told him he could share what he was comfortable with when he was ready. He'd told them a little after a while, but never shared much. Thought it was better all around to just let the past go. He definitely never intended on sharing this part of his past. But with Bailey turning up out of nowhere, looking like she did, he didn't have much of a choice now.

"I...like I said, we were working together," he admitted. "She was just getting her start, and I took her under my wing. I was a sergeant in the Kings Mountain Police Department at the time, and I could see something in her, even though we were just working in a small town. The other guys on the force, none of them had anything on her. She had good instincts, always knew how to handle herself, even when things got hard. That's why I..."

He trailed off again. Crap. He didn't know if it was safe to talk to them about this, even after all this time. He had done such a good job of putting it all behind him, it almost felt wrong to dredge it all up like this. But now that Bailey had appeared in his life again, he needed to find out what was going on with her. He had to get to the bottom of what brought her to Warrior Peak looking for him.

"I thought I knew the guys we were working with," he explained as best he could. "Usual small-town cop stuff, you know. That was, until I found out there was way more going on in that department than I had realized."

"Like?" Lawson prompted.

"Like...they were covering stuff up," he continued. "Hiding things, making sure certain information about certain investigations was lost so they could keep their contacts out of prison…bribery, threats. I had started looking into closed cases, some things that seemed suspicious, coincidences that just didn't add up. I was getting close, but didn't have time to get to the bottom of it all before they started to figure out that I was on to them. I guess they had their own suspicions and had someone watching me…and Bailey."

His gut clenched at the thought. Even now, he could still remember the night when they had confronted him about what he knew. When they had cornered him at his car, he thought they might be fishing for information, maybe toss out a threat, throw a punch or two.

When Ziegler had pinned him against his car and the others closed in, he knew they were out for blood.

They beat the hell out of him. Busted ribs, a concussion, and a slew of cuts and bruises. He could empathize with Bailey's condition right now. And that alone would have been bad enough to make Aaron rethink what he was doing, just for his own safety. But he would have still stayed if it wasn't for the threat they made to Bailey.

We could take her out in a second if you don't get out of town, and pretend none of this ever happened. You understand?

Even the thought of it had been enough to scare him. He hadn't realized how deeply he cared for her until he was faced with the thought of losing her. He knew he couldn't let it happen. He cared for her way too deeply, and he needed to know she was safe.

And while she could handle herself, she couldn't take an attack at the level he had just suffered. She was so vulnerable, and she didn't even know it. He hadn't told her a thing about his investigation, not wanting to involve her until he had something solid to go on.

And so, he'd fled town. But first, he had written a scathing report about Bailey and left it on his captain's desk. Something that he knew would get her sent to another department and stuck behind a desk instead of out in the field and in harm's way. He'd felt horrible writing those disparaging words about her performance, but at least he knew she'd be safe from the corruption and threats. That mattered more to him than her feelings. He filled Lawson and Xavier in on the story as quickly as he could. When he was done, Lawson let out a long whistle between his teeth.

"No wonder she was chewing you out earlier." He shook his head. "She thinks you just turned on her out of nowhere. I would be mad, too."

"Yeah," Aaron muttered, hoping her anger would fade. Surely, it had to, if she was here to get help, right? He knew she wasn't safe, and he had a sneaking suspicion that the same guys who had caused so much chaos in his own life were the ones behind her problems now.

"So what do you think she's doing here?" Xavier asked, frowning. "Must have been something serious if she was willing to put aside what you did to her to come here."

"Yeah, it must have been," Aaron agreed. He could still see in his mind's eye the way she had looked at him when he had asked her who'd done this to her—the split second of vulnerability, covered up by how much she hated him and what he had done to her. Did she have any idea why? It was all part of the process of protecting her from those men. Without him, she would've been easy pickings for them. Either she would have been forced to join their corrupt circle, or they'd have disposed of her in any way they saw fit. Neither option sounded like a good one to Aaron at the time.

"So, from what happened to you, you think the same guys are after her now?" Xavier continued, crossing his arms over his chest. "You know how important it is that we keep this place secure. Especially after what happened when Cade brought River here—"

"I know, I know," Aaron replied, nodding. It had been a safe space for him when he had needed it most, and he was going to do his best to ensure it stayed that way. He just needed to get Bailey to talk to him, to confirm what he already thought to be true.

He wasn't the only one either. Aaron knew exactly what Xavier was referring to—when Cade had stopped to help a woman on the side of the road. He'd given her a ride to Warrior Peak and they had ended up falling in love, and then her past had caught up with her. She'd had her own dark stuff to face, but with the help of Cade and the others there at the lodge, she'd done it. Now, River, the woman treating Bailey right now, was an essential part of Warrior Peak Sanctuary.

AARON HADN'T BEEN aware of all the details regarding Cade and River because he had kept to himself in the background. He had been busy trying to escape his own past rather than getting involved with others. He would never forgive himself, though, if his presence at the sanctuary compromised the safety of others again.

"So you need to find out who did this to her," Lawson added, with a scowl. "I don't care what happened between the two of you in the past. What matters now is the present, and we need to have all the information we can upfront so we know what we might be dealing with."

"I'll do my best once she's patched up," Aaron promised, hoping they believed him. He had been working here for the better part of six years, and it had earned him a little grace—they hadn't turned Bailey away when she had come asking for him, after all. But that was only going to last so long. If he couldn't get some information out of her soon, there was going to be trouble.

"You want a coffee while you wait?" Xavier asked, jerking his head toward the cafeteria.

"No, I'm going to wait here," he replied.

Xavier paused for a moment, clearly about to add something, but then thought better of it. "Okay, fill us in on what you find out as soon as she's settled," he said instead. Then he and Lawson walked away, leaving Aaron alone with his thoughts once more.

He shot a look toward the door, wondering if Bailey would let him come in right now. He just wanted to see her. Being so close to her again after all this time was almost surreal, like something out of a dream. She had been such a big part of his life for so long, but he'd had to sever the ties between them bluntly and brutally with no explanation. Even if she did end up with a better understanding of what had happened, would it be enough to convince her to forgive him?

And what if this had something to do with the corruption he'd discovered before? What if she had walked back into the middle of it and found herself faced with a harsh reality she wasn't ready for? She was a principled woman, always had been, and she wouldn't have stood for that kind of behavior in any of her colleagues. But her principles wouldn't have been enough to keep her safe if they turned on her, and he hated the thought of something happening to her. Maybe if he had told her the truth back then…

He tried to push the thought to the back of his mind. He couldn't obsess over what had happened before—that was in the past now. All he could do was focus on the present, and how he was going to get her to tell him who had hurt her and why. She might have been more willing to speak with one of the other women there, but he needed something to report back to Lawson and Xavier. They wouldn't want her here if she refused to tell them the truth. He understood why.

He and Bailey had shared a real trust back in the day, and he just needed to find some way to tap into that again. He had missed her every single day since he had walked away from his old life. Seeing her again brought up a million of the old emotions he had done his best to forget.

But things were different now. He just had to find some way to handle whatever came next, and make sure she didn't end up with any more dangerous injuries in the process.

He looked once more at the door, then began to pace again while he waited. He had a feeling it was going to be a long day.

Chapter Five

When Bailey's eyes opened again, it took her a minute to remember where she was. She sat upright as quickly as her sore body would allow, and looked around.

"Hey, you're awake. Take it easy, you don't want to move around too fast," a soothing voice said on her left.

She looked over to see the woman who had been tending to her. She was sipping on coffee and sitting in a chair against the wall.

"What's going on?" Bailey mumbled, a little disorientated. The pain was better, but she was feeling a bit sick from the blood loss and lack of food. She actually didn't remember when she ate last, but she needed to get something in her soon. Plus, she had no idea who this woman who had been watching her sleep was. She seemed friendly enough, but she was a stranger. She kind of assumed Aaron would be there with her, waiting for answers.

"You passed out," the woman replied gently. "I was looking after you while you were resting. I've patched you up and gave you some painkillers, too."

Bailey tried to sit up straighter while keeping the woman in sight. She noticed the pain in her ribs was not as intense, and her leg wasn't throbbing as much. So that was something, at least.

"I'm River." The woman introduced herself. "I work here at Warrior Peak Sanctuary."

"Are you a doctor?" Bailey couldn't see a reason why this woman would be here looking after her otherwise.

"No, but I do have some medical experience. When someone's hurt, the guys usually get me first to see if it's something easily treatable before they call the town doctor or discuss going to the hospital."

That made sense. And Bailey was grateful for the assistance. There was no way she wanted to go into town, and definitely not to a hospital. That would lead them right to her.

"Well, thank you, River. I appreciate you helping me," Bailey replied, and she meant it. Even though she was exhausted and sore, her gut told her that she was in a safe place. That she didn't have to worry about those men finding her while she was here.

"You know much about Warrior Peak Sanctuary?" River asked.

Bailey shook her head slowly, noting that it didn't feel as bad as before, either. She hadn't known anything about this place, apart from the fact that Aaron worked here. That was the only reason she had come. On the run, she had only been able to think of one person she could trust, even if he was also the last person on earth she wanted to see.

"It used to be for law enforcement and military people who'd suffered through traumatic events and were recovering, but it's expanding now," she explained with a soft smile. "It's also for people getting out of dangerous situations who need a place to stay while they get back on their feet. So you're safe here. I promise. These are good guys and they just want to help."

Bailey nodded. There was a note of sincerity in River's voice, and she wondered if she had been through something similar—something crazy that had brought her here in the first place.

"And speaking of traumatic situations," she added, nodding toward Bailey. "You really got yourself beat up. In case you're unaware, you have a few cracked ribs and a stab wound on your thigh. I'd like to check you for a concussion, too, considering that goose egg you've got on your head."

"Sounds about right." Bailey sighed. The attack was still something of a blur to her, but she remembered hands on her, the flash of metal, the terror she felt in that instant, certain this was the end for her.

"You mind?" River indicated toward Bailey's head.

Bailey nodded slowly. "Sure. Go ahead. I don't think I have one, though."

"Let's just double-check to be certain," she replied, then asked Bailey to follow her directions as she examined her head further. Once she was satisfied there was no concussion, she sat back in her chair, giving Bailey space. "You want to tell me what happened?" she asked.

Bailey flattened her lips and shook her head at once. River might have seemed nice, but she didn't know a damn thing about her, and she wasn't about to go handing over her biggest secrets without getting to know her a little better. If these last couple of days had taught her anything, it was that she couldn't exactly trust everyone she thought she could. She needed to be way more careful about how she handled herself.

"No problem. I get it," River murmured, and she rose to her feet. "You stay put. I'm going to see if dinner is ready. You must be starving, and getting some nourishment and fluids in you will help you feel a bit better. We usually eat together in the cafeteria, but I don't think you're in any state to be getting up right now."

Bailey thanked her again, and let out a sigh of relief as soon as River closed the door behind her. She squeezed her eyes shut and tried to remind herself that she was here for one person and one person only—Aaron. She had to get the truth out of him. She was sure he must have known something about the nightmare that had driven her out here. Maybe it even had something to do with his sudden departure.

She was regretting how she had handled seeing him again. She shouldn't have blown up at him like she did. It wasn't her best move, going on the attack, when he was who she was here to see. Telling him to leave her alone and she'd handle it wasn't exactly her brightest moment. He must think she'd lost her mind. She needed to get herself under control before she saw him again.

River returned with another woman in tow, carrying three plates of food between them. River handed one to Bailey, who took it gratefully. It was just meat and veggies, nothing special, but to her hungry stomach, it looked like a damn cornucopia.

"This is Hannah." River introduced the other woman, who smiled kindly in greeting. Bailey vaguely remembered seeing her when she had rushed in the building asking for Aaron.

"Hi there. If you need anything while you're here, let me know. I tend to have the most interactions with the guests with their day-to-day needs. The guys are more involved with keeping the place running and the bigger problems."

"Thanks, I'll keep that in mind." Though Bailey had no idea how long she'd be here.

"I also heard your meeting with Aaron earlier didn't go too well," Hannah remarked. "So, I figured you would probably want some space to yourself to regroup and rest instead of going to sit with everyone else for dinner."

"Yeah, thanks," Bailey replied. These women were being so kind to her, but all she could think about right now was Aaron.

"So how many people usually stay here?" she asked, keeping her voice as casual as possible. She didn't want these women thinking she was trying to scope the place out, though that was exactly her intention. She needed to know how many people she was looking at, and then she could figure out where to go from there.

"Anywhere from ten to twenty on average," Hannah replied through a mouthful of food. "It's pretty busy in the cafeteria in the evenings, as everyone eats together."

"Well, thanks for giving me an out from that," she replied. She appreciated it. The thought of being around so many people she didn't know was discomforting right now, to say the least, especially after what had happened to her. Her instincts radar seemed to be malfunctioning.

"Hey, I get it," Hannah replied. "Most people who come here need a little time to themselves at first. It's not unusual."

She paused for a moment, staring at Bailey, and then exchanged a glance with River.

"So," she said, "how long are you planning on staying, exactly?"

Bailey didn't know. These women were being so nice to her and they hadn't asked her to leave, but she wasn't sure how to respond. She knew they were curious as to why she was here in the first place, broken and beaten no less. She wasn't sure what she could tell them that wouldn't guarantee more questions she couldn't answer. Not yet, anyway.

"Until I get what I came here for," she replied firmly. That was something, right? Enough for them to go on for now.

"And what did you come here for?" Hannah inquired.

"To get information from Aaron," she muttered, more to herself than to the other women. And with that, she turned her attention back to her food, shutting off the conversation before it could go any further.

Once they had finished dinner, River and Hannah cleared out and left Bailey to get some rest, much to her relief. She was exhausted, and her body still ached, despite the pain meds. She tried to remind herself that this wouldn't last forever—she would get better soon.

Right now, she just needed to rest and work on rebuilding her strength. Hopefully, they'd let her do that here. She could feel her eyelids getting heavy as she snuggled down under the covers.

She drifted off with thoughts of Aaron and the last time they were together before her life went to shambles.

Answers first, then she'd maybe see if there was anything left of them to salvage.

She startled awake and it took her a minute to realize where she was. Looking around the room, she felt everything come rushing back. Kings Mountain, her attack, finding Aaron, Warrior Peak Sanctuary. She suddenly felt like the walls were beginning to close in on her.

It was dark outside, and she didn't hear any activity or voices inside, but she needed to get out of this room. She slowly rose to her feet, even as her body screamed in protest, and silently opened the bedroom door. The painkillers were starting to wear off, but she didn't care. She needed some fresh air. Hopefully, it was late enough that she wasn't going to run into anyone.

She made her way through the quiet corridors of the lodge, half expecting to bump into someone, but found the place empty. She took a couple of wrong turns, but eventually managed to find the lobby. She stepped outside the main entrance and inhaled a big lungful of fresh air. Her ribs protested, but the stretch still felt good. She wasn't used to lying in a prone position for so long. It was colder up here on the mountain, she realized. The air felt crisper, cleaner.

In the distance, she saw the trees swaying in the breeze, the sound of the leaves rustling the only noise around her. Her back still ached like crazy, and she knew she wasn't going to be able to take a walk or anything like that, but at least she could get out of that room and try to clear her head.

She had no idea what she was going to do, now that she was here. Get the truth from Aaron, sure, but what then? She didn't have a clue. She was in no condition to go back to work, and even if she did, those corrupt cops in the department wouldn't allow it. If she ever showed her face around there again, she wasn't sure she would walk away with her life this time. She wasn't sure why she had now. The thought sent a shiver down her spine.

She spotted a small porch seat around the side of the building, and she slowly made her way to it, glad to take the weight off her injured leg. She hated feeling this weak. She might be small, but she had always prided herself on being strong and fit. To be enfeebled and injured was an awful feeling. She wanted to heal so she could take on the men who had done this to her. She wanted to expose them for everything they had done, not just to her but to the community. But right now, she couldn't have won a fight against a kitten.

She heard footsteps behind her, and without even having to turn around, she knew at once who it was. A weight landed on the seat next to her, and she smelled his cologne, the familiar scent of him that she had grown to love so much when they had been working together.

"What are you doing out here?" Aaron asked her. "You should be resting."

She didn't reply. She wasn't going to take orders from him, and she didn't feel like arguing. He wasn't her boss or even her friend, anymore. Nobody who really cared about her could ever have done something like he did, no matter the reasons.

But, as she felt the warmth radiating from his body, she knew she didn't have it in her to ask to be left alone. He was the reason she had come to this place. As much as she didn't want to admit it, she needed him. It would have been a whole lot easier if she could just forget about him, but that was never going to work.

"You mind if I sit with you?" he asked, and she shook her head.

"No." She sighed. She missed this, his closeness. There had been a time when they had known everything about each other—or so she'd thought.

"How are you doing?" he asked.

Her shoulders slumped slightly. "About as well as I can be, given that I was just beaten up by a bunch of dirty cops."

She felt the air shift between them at once. Was he expecting her to say that? Hoping she wouldn't? She didn't have a clue. She stole a look at him out of the corner of her eye, wishing she could just ask him what was going on in his head, but she had to be more careful than that. She had let this man close to her once before, and it had ended with her getting burned. She wasn't going to hand him the chance to do that to her again.

"What happened?" he asked her.

Rubbing her hand over her face, and trying to ignore the sharp twinge in her ribs, she reasoned with herself. She came to this place to find him, ask for his help. She had to tell him at some point so she could get answers. So, why not here? Why not now?

Chapter Six

Aaron's mind was reeling as he took in what she had just said. Dirty cops? The same ones he had dealt with? They had to be, right? There was no way she could have encountered anyone else. His skin crawled when he thought about what they might have done to her, but the best he could do right now was listen.

"I... I finally got out from under the curse you put on me," she snapped back. She was still defensive, but at least she was talking. It was a start.

"What do you mean?"

"When you got me sent out to the middle of nowhere to be stuck behind a desk all day?" she reminded him sarcastically, as though he might have forgotten. "I just spent the last six years there. Trust me, I've been counting every day."

The bitterness in her voice was obvious, and he hated hearing her so angry at him. But she had a right to be. He needed to give her the time to come to terms with it, because six years still hadn't been enough.

"I finally worked hard enough to convince them to put me back out in the field," she explained. "And there was only one place I wanted to do it. Kings Mountain."

His heart sank. So she had walked right back into all

of that? With no warning? And he was sure Ziegler and the others would have gotten bolder with what they were doing, willing to push the boundaries even further than they had when he was there.

"I got a warm welcome, let's just say that," she remarked. "From Ziegler in particular."

Aaron felt a flare of rage in his system, as he thought about how vulnerable she must have been, and how quick they had been to make a move on her.

"How long were you back before it started?"

"It was the first night," she replied. "I wasn't set to work until the next day, but I was excited to be back. Dropped by the station to check in and say hi to everyone. They were the first ones who greeted me and asked me out for a drink to celebrate my return." She paused, and shivered like she was reliving it in her mind.

He clenched his fists at his sides to keep from reaching for her. "What happened?" he asked again.

"Everything was fine, at first. Then they started talking smack about you. It caught me off guard and when they turned the questions to me...how far I was willing to go to keep my job, stuff like that... I panicked and rushed out. They didn't hold back. I thought they were going to kill me," she whispered.

She paused again and wrapped her arms around herself, her gaze distant. Aaron slid closer to her, offering his warmth and silent support.

"I barely remember the attack," she murmured. "They had followed me out of the bar and ganged up on me in the parking lot when I was trying to leave. I had just made it to my truck when they shoved my head into the side of it. I vaguely remember hands tugging on me, someone yanked my head back, I think. The glint of a knife..." She trailed off and shuddered. "I woke up in a lot of pain and bleeding on the ground."

Aaron winced but didn't say anything, allowing her to continue.

"When I regained consciousness, I jumped in my truck and took off. I didn't even really know where I was going. I just wanted to put as much distance as possible between myself and those guys." She took a shaky breath and shrugged. "I drove home, threw some things in a bag, then I ended up here looking for you...and you know the rest."

"I'm so sorry this happened to you, Bailey," he said softly.

She looked at him out of the corner of her eye. "You knew about it, right?" she asked.

He nodded. No point in trying to hide it now. The truth was out, and she was in danger. No matter how much he wished he could undo what had happened to her, there was no walking away from this.

"Yeah, I did," he replied apologetically. "I was looking into them, trying to collect evidence to take to the captain. Apparently, they had their own suspicions about me and confronted me. Anyway, I'm glad you found me, but how did you know where I was?"

"Because *they* knew where you were. Lee specifically mentioned this place. That's how I knew where to come. They must have searched for you after you left."

Those words hung in the air for a moment as he processed them. They knew? For how long? Why hadn't they come to find him yet?

"Right," he murmured. He had no idea what to say to

that. Whether she knew it or not, she was admitting that he was in danger—that both of them were. This wasn't a safe place for him anymore. The thought of Warrior Peak being compromised, of bringing more danger to the door of the people who had offered him sanctuary when he had needed it most made him feel sick.

"I'm going to stay here as long it takes me to get back on my feet," she told him, stretching her arms above her head and wincing. Her shirt rode up, revealing the bruising on her sides, and he clenched his fists when he thought about who must have done that to her. All of them ganging up on this woman? Four big men against one small woman. It was totally disgusting. She was lucky to have made it out alive, though he was sure he didn't need to remind her of that.

"And then I'm going back, and I'm going to bring them to justice," she added, narrowing her eyes. "Just because you could ignore it for six years, doesn't mean I can."

The jab stung. He had only left that place without doing more to stop them because he had known how much danger it would put her in, but he didn't know if she was ready to hear it. Or if she would even believe him if he told her. He wished he could just get her to trust him somehow, but he had broken that trust before and he wasn't sure what it would take for them to put the pieces back together again.

She rose to her feet, or at least tried to. She needed to lean heavily on the porch railing to get herself back upright, and he stood up and offered her a hand.

"You need some help?" he asked her, and she fired him a look and snorted.

"You really think I need help from you?" she demanded, raising her eyebrows. "All you've ever done is cause me trouble."

"All I've ever done?" he echoed.

Something in her face shifted as she looked away. "Not...not all you've ever done," she admitted, lowering her gaze to the ground. "When we were working together, Aaron, that was the happiest I'd ever been. I know I was young, but I...the connection we had, it was real. And then for you to turn and do that to me, without any warning, without giving me any chance to stand up for myself..." She trailed off, her eyes shining with tears for a moment. "I just didn't get it."

She shrugged, her eyes becoming guarded again. He wanted to reach out and take her hand, tell her that he had felt the same way about her, but he'd had to make a hard choice to try to protect her. And that he would have done anything he could to not hurt her, but the situation was so complicated.

"I looked up to you so much," she admitted. "And I wanted you to notice me as more than just a rookie, you know?"

Aaron knew exactly what she meant, and he wished he could tell her that he did—he had seen her as so much more than just her job. He had gotten to know her deeply, and the bond they had shared—beyond just a professional connection—was something he had never found since. She paused for a moment before she kept talking, her mind clearly racing.

"I would have believed you, you know," she told him, shaking her head. "I would have believed you if you'd come to me and told me what was going on in the department. I don't know what you were trying to protect me from, but you didn't need to do all of that to look out for me."

A million words were on the tip of his tongue, but he couldn't find a way to get any of them out that would actually make a difference. He knew she was mad at him. She probably would be for the rest of her life. They had worked so closely together, and now she was being faced with the reality of what had driven them apart. She didn't know every detail yet, but he was sure she would insist on getting to the bottom of it.

She hobbled toward the door and went inside. Aaron thought about going after her, but he knew it wouldn't have led to anything good. She still wasn't in a place where she could talk to him, but it looked as though she was going to be sticking around for a while as she got back on her feet. Maybe they would get a chance to talk while she was recovering.

Even though he was tired, he sank back down on to the porch seat and stared out into the forest beyond. The news she had given him, that they knew where he was, changed everything. He was going to have to find some way to protect himself, and this place.

Soon enough, he'd have to tell Xavier and Lawson about it, even though he wished he could find any way out of that damn conversation. He knew they were going to all but put this place on lockdown, and the thought of bringing that kind of stress to their door just didn't sit right with him.

But he didn't have a choice. Even if it would change this place that had been his safe haven. It had been so long, he had gotten comfortable—stopped looking over his shoulder and started to actually feel like he belonged here. He never expected his past to put the lodge—and the people who lived here—in danger. And he definitely never expected to see Bailey again after what had happened.

When he thought of what Bailey must have been through, he couldn't help but feel guilty. He had left her to that, whether he had meant to or not. He should have known that she would work her way back on to the streets again—she was too good to sit behind a desk. One negative report from him wasn't going to be enough to get the people around her to ignore the work she did. She had never been the kind of person to leave something unfinished, so he should have known she'd want to go back to Kings Mountain. He'd completely left her unprepared for what she'd face if she did.

But back then, he had hardly been able to think past getting her out of there. Thinking about her at all had been too painful for him, so imagining what would have come next for her was something he couldn't even let himself do. He had hoped she was safe, that she was happy, that she didn't hate him. But since she had walked back into his life, it was clear that none of that applied.

She'd admitted that she had feelings for him when they were first working together, and his head was still spinning as he tried to wrap his mind around it. He had never imagined she would have looked at him that way. Would he have acted on it then, if he'd known? He wanted to believe he was better than that, but his attraction to her had been intense.

It still was, if he was honest with himself. Even when she was as beaten down as she was, she was still fiercely captivating. She was still the woman he remembered from all those years ago, but this time, more sure of herself, with more life experience behind her.

And, when she was faced with danger, she still came looking for him. After all this time, she still sought him out. Obviously, even if she didn't seem willing to admit it right now, some part of her still felt safe with him.

He hoped he could do that part of her proud.

He had made peace with the fact that she was going to hate him after he wrote that report. But now that she was back in his life, he didn't know if he could live with it. He didn't want her walking around here, loathing him for his betrayal, when it was so much more complicated than that. Look at the state she was in now—it would have been even worse if they had launched this attack on her when she had been a rookie, without him there to cover for her.

The moon was high in the sky, bathing everything around Aaron in a bright glow. It was peaceful out here for now, but that was all going to change soon enough. Now that they knew where he was, his days of peace and quiet were over.

And he had to be ready for whatever came next.

Chapter Seven

Bailey eased herself out of bed, not wanting to move too quickly. She knew she had to give herself time to rest, no matter how tempting it might have been to just force herself to get back out there and pick up where she had left off.

After nearly a week here, she finally felt like she was getting her feet back under her again. Though she had mostly kept out of the way of the people milling around, she had been getting to know the horses that lived out behind the main lodge in the paddock. Hannah had told her that they were a relatively new arrival. They helped some of the people who had a hard time dealing with other humans. Bailey could see exactly what the appeal was—she didn't have to hide herself or worry about what she said around them, she could just relax.

She had formed a particular bond with Wheatie, an old palomino mare who had been taken in by them when her old owners had gotten too frail to care for her. She was incredibly gentle, and had started rushing up to the fence whenever she saw Bailey getting close, clearly not willing to let her get away without seeing if she had an apple tucked in her pocket for her first.

In fact, that was exactly where Bailey was headed

right after breakfast. She tried to arrive at the cafeteria a little after everyone else, so she didn't have to worry about too many questions, and it was nearly empty by the time she got there today. Good. She hadn't seen Aaron in a few days, and she wasn't ready to talk to him again, not after their last conversation. She just needed a little more time to shore up her defenses before facing him again. That's why she'd been avoiding him.

She knew she had laid too much on the line, right there on her first night. She should have been more careful, held a little more back, but she couldn't stand the thought of him not knowing how much she had cared for him back then. He hadn't trusted her with the truth, but she would have listened to him—she wouldn't have shut him down or told him he was crazy. And she would have worked to bring those corrupt cops down right alongside him.

Confessing her once deeply held feelings for him felt like a risk she wasn't sure she should have taken. What was he going to think of her now? Had he felt the same way? Even if he'd had feelings for her back then, he had still betrayed her. Her heart still hurt when she thought of what he had done to her, and the fact he was capable of it. She didn't know if she could trust him again, but she knew she'd have to try.

Once she'd had breakfast, she headed out to the paddock, carrying her weight on her uninjured leg. The pain was still there, but it had improved a whole lot. River had tried to convince her to get checked out at a local hospital, but she had turned her down, not wanting to leave a paper trail so she could be tracked. She was sure the cops who had done this to her would be searching for her already, and she didn't need to make it any easier for them than she already had.

She had been convinced by Hannah to see Carter, one of the physical therapists. Carter's brother, Cade, had made sure to give him a glowing recommendation and passed it along to Hannah and the guys saying how much Carter had helped him when he first came to the lodge.

She reached the field and saw Wheatie trotting over to greet her, her mane bouncing with every step. Bailey couldn't help but grin, but the smile soon faded from her face when she spotted Aaron working on a fence at the edge of the paddock.

He glanced up and saw her coming before she could turn to leave, and he waved her over. Wheatie diverted her attention to him, nuzzling her head into his shoulder, and he reached over to stroke her nose.

"How are you doing?" he asked Bailey.

"I'm fine," Bailey answered, even as a bolt of pain traveled up the length of her leg. Ugh, she hated this. She wished she didn't have to deal with him right now. Being around him was so damn confusing, her head going in a million different directions at once. And she was embarrassed that she had been so vulnerable with him on her first night there.

"You sure about that?" he asked, watching as she leaned on the fence to take the weight off her leg.

She nodded. "Sure. You know, I never asked what you do around here."

He smirked slightly at her sudden change of subject. He paused for a moment, debating whether to let her off the hook before replying. "I got hired as Warrior Peak's handyman. Kind of a jack-of-all-trades, help wherever's needed."

"Ah, so how long you been up here?" she asked, directing her attention back to the horse.

"Been here around six years. A friend in the department had used this place to recover after he suffered injuries in an undercover sting operation. Said it was a good place to contemplate and re-evaluate life choices. Figured it wouldn't hurt to give it a try." He paused for a moment before he continued. Let her read into that what she will. He still didn't think she was ready to hear everything yet. "So...what do you know about Ziegler and the rest of the guys?"

She shrugged. "Not much. Definitely never would have thought they were dirty cops."

"How did it all happen?" he pressed, leaning forward with interest. "Did they try to get you on board, or—"

"No, no, nothing like that," she replied. "Like I said before, they invited me out for a drink to celebrate, and everything seemed normal, at first. They all seemed happy to have me back. And then I asked about you. You were the elephant in the room, after all, so I thought I'd just rip off the Band-Aid and move on. But one of them said something and the atmosphere of the place shifted. Something about you being a rat, then their friendly tones changed to more menacing and made me uncomfortable. So I threw out an excuse and left, and they followed me out."

His shoulders slumped as he took in what she was saying, as though he was blaming himself for it. Maybe he was. He was the one who had hidden it from her, after all. If she had known what she was walking into, she would have been better prepared to handle it.

"I'm sorry you had to go through that," he replied.

She frowned. "I think they could tell there was no chance I was ever going to go along with their corruption, so they had to get rid of me or scare me into silence. Now that I know what I'm dealing with, it's going to be a lot easier," she remarked. She could already feel herself shifting back into cop mode.

"What's going to be easier?"

"They were so impulsive…so reckless," she continued on, as if he hadn't spoken. "They've gotten away with their operation for so long that they're cocky, Aaron. There's no way they haven't made mistakes. We just have to find one and expose them. I know there's something—we just need to find it."

"We?" he replied, cocking an eyebrow.

She shrugged. "I can tell you're still a cop, under all of this," she replied, gesturing to his clothes. "The sergeant who trained me is still in there."

"I left the force for a reason," he muttered.

She shot him a look. "Yeah, I know you did," she replied. "Because you didn't think you could take those guys on by yourself. But you're not going to have to. We can do this together. I know we can."

Wheatie snorted, as though agreeing with her. She reached out to pet the horse, running her fingers through her silken mane.

"You should just let me handle this," he replied. "Like I should have done six years ago."

She shook her head at once. "I'm not letting you deal with this all alone again. That was the problem the first time around," she pointed out. "But we can't just let them get away with this. Think about how many people they must have hurt over the years, how many victims have gone without justice. I can't just walk away from this. Even if you could."

He winced. It was a low blow, and she knew it. But she wouldn't apologize. He should have stood up and fought all those years ago, even if it meant putting himself in danger. She had always seen him as a principled, passionate cop, but to know he had left without trying to do more made her doubt all of that.

He seemed to be able to tell that he wasn't going to change her mind, and he checked one of the nails in the fence before he replied.

"At least stay here while we work out a plan," he suggested. "That way, I know you're safe."

"You're sure you don't want to send me away again?" she fired back. "Maybe Florida this time?"

He glared at her, a flash of anger in his eyes. "You know I did the best I could at the time."

"Your best wasn't good enough," she spat back, even though she knew she was being unfair. She couldn't make herself care. Everything in her life seemed unfair right now, and she needed to take it out on someone. Since he was partly to blame, he was her target. If he'd only confided in her, let her help…

He took a step toward her, his eyes blazing. "You don't get to decide that," he told her. "If you had any idea of what I'd been up against—"

"I would have helped you!" she protested, shaking

her head. "I would have done everything I could have to work with you and bring those guys down, you know that. You didn't give me the choice. You got me shipped off to the middle of nowhere because you thought you knew what was best for me."

"I wasn't going to let them target you!" he exclaimed. It was the most emotion she had seen from him since she'd shown up at the sanctuary. Even though it was more anger than anything else, it was a relief to see him as emotional about this as she was. Her whole life had been torn apart—the man she had admired, maybe even loved, had betrayed her. He couldn't expect her to just forget about it and move on, even all these years later.

"I cared about you too much to put you in the line of fire," he said.

"And I cared about you too much to believe you could do something like that to me," she snapped back. "You threw me aside like I was nothing. Like I was a bad cop. How was I supposed to feel?"

He opened his mouth like he was going to answer, but clamped it shut again with a sigh. He looked away like he would rather be doing anything else except having this conversation. But they would have to talk about it sooner or later. Better to get it over with now.

He scrubbed a hand down his face. "I wanted to keep you safe, and that was the only way I could think of to do it. I didn't have a lot of time to think through options," he told her. "It wasn't what I wanted. I never wanted you to hate me."

"What did you want?" she demanded.

For a split second, she could feel it between them again—that heat, the chemistry she had tried to deny for so long. It was like they were back in his cruiser, the two of them bantering over some case, just like they had back in the old days.

He took a deep breath and looked at the sky. "You."

Chapter Eight

Bailey just stared at him for a moment. Disbelief crossed her face. She drew in a sharp breath, just like she used to do when he took a corner a little too fast in the cruiser when they were on the move. He could still remember the way she shifted in her seat, how her hand would reach for the dashboard to balance herself. She was normally so composed, but those flashes of what was underneath always intrigued him.

And the times she had reached over to grab his arm to steady herself. He could still remember that feeling, her fingertips digging into his skin, how it made him feel like he belonged there. How he never wanted to be anywhere but by her side.

"You can't say that," she replied finally, her voice a little shaky. "It's not fair—"

"It's the truth," he replied. "What else do you want me to say? I wanted you, Bailey. And I wanted you to be safe above all else. I could never have forgiven myself if something had happened to you. That's why I did what I did."

He spoke fervently, meaning every word—every word he wished he could have said to her all those years ago, before he'd had to turn his back on her the way he had.

He had lost so much because of Ziegler and his cronies, but worse, so had Bailey, and she hadn't had a choice in the matter.

"I know it feels like I betrayed you. I don't blame you for feeling that way," he continued. "But I... I couldn't have lived with myself if something had happened, and I knew I could have stopped it. Coming here, sending you away, they were last-minute decisions and the only things I could think of right then. I didn't exactly have a lot of space to put together a plan."

Bailey pushed her fingers through Wheatie's mane again, not looking at him, but clearly listening. She grimaced and began massaging her thigh around her wound, clearly still in quite a bit of pain.

"Here, let me help," he said, stepping forward and holding out an arm to lean on.

"I don't need your help," she muttered.

"I would do the same for anyone," he replied, and she reluctantly put a hand on his shoulder to steady herself as she waited for the pain to subside again. Her proximity was bringing up more feelings than he knew what to do with, so he swiftly shifted the conversation to something a little less loaded.

"How have the last few years been for you, anyway?" he asked. "I mean, besides hating my guts."

She sighed, like she didn't want to talk about it. He half expected her to just turn around and leave, and maybe she would have if her leg wasn't hurting her so badly. But instead, she answered him.

"Life wasn't all bad out there," she replied. "I loved being next to the ocean. And I got to know some cool people in the Bay, too—they were sad when I left, actually. I thought about sticking around there, but I had to go back to Kings Mountain. That was where it all started for me. Felt like a full circle moment."

She shook her head.

"Maybe I should have just accepted that my career in North Carolina was over," she added. "None of this would have happened if I had just stayed put."

"Yeah, but you were always stubborn," he added, as she shifted her hand back to the fence.

"I wasn't that bad," she protested.

He laughed. "Bailey, remember I worked with you," he reminded her. "I saw all the sides of you. And how hard it was for you to let go of anything, even when it would have been a better idea."

Kind of like she was doing now, actually. If she had been smart, she would have seen that there was no reason to keep pushing to get to the bottom of this corruption scandal. They were small-time, and it would likely just cause her more suffering in the long term. But she had made her mind up, and when she made her mind up, there was no stopping her.

"Maybe I've changed," she remarked. "I had to learn a lot of patience working behind a desk all that time."

"Maybe you have," he agreed, though he wasn't sure he believed it.

He could tell by the way she carried herself she was the same Bailey he had known from all those years ago—the same woman filled with ambition and a sense of justice that ran deep down inside of her. These guys didn't know what they were up against. Getting Bailey involved in all of this might have been the biggest mistake they had ever made.

But, judging by the state of her now, it might cost her more.

"What about you?" she asked, turning the question around on him.

"What about me?"

She gestured around the paddock. "You always seemed like such a cop to me. You must have been going crazy up here, bored all this time."

"It's not as bad as all that," he replied. "Not anymore, at least."

He had struggled when he'd first arrived, trying to adapt to this new reality and this version of himself that wasn't a cop. The version of himself that wasn't out on the beat doing everything he could to make the world a safer place.

"It's been a good change of pace," he continued. "I get to help people here. I still feel like I'm doing some good. And the people who run this place, they're damn good guys. I'm grateful they gave me a purpose after I…"

He trailed off. No point in finishing that sentence. After he had given up his old purpose? That was what he really felt like saying. He had walked away from everything he had known, and getting settled here had been tough. He could still remember those first few restless months, feeling like he had made a mistake and wondering how long he could stick this out. Wondering if he could turn back time and undo what he had done, though he knew it was far too late for that.

"Never thought I would see you settle down, especially not in a place like this," she added. "It's just a plot of land in the middle of nowhere."

"That's what it looks like from the outside," he agreed.

"But there's way more to it than that. Way more to everyone here, too. Everyone has their stories. Either they're running away from something, or they're searching for their own purpose. I guess I was a little of both."

"Guess so," she agreed, and he saw the flicker of a smile pass over her lips. He missed that smile, more than he would have cared to admit to himself. Seeing it again made his chest tighten. He shifted his gaze from her, not wanting to stare for too long. Their history was too long and messy now to let anything romantic get in the way. Even if he wished things were different.

"It's like it settles into you as you settle into it," he explained. "I didn't think I would like it here as much as I do, but the longer I stayed, the more I liked it. Maybe you'll find the same thing, too."

"Maybe," she replied with a shrug, as though she didn't really believe him. "You think you'll ever leave?"

He looked around at the paddock, Wheatie, and the other horses gallivanting around happily. This place was so far removed from his old life, it was hard to even imagine what being a cop had been like. Yes, there were times when he missed it, but this place had become his new home, and he didn't want to change that.

He shook his head. "I don't think so."

He was surprised by his answer, but it felt right. There was a time when he would have jumped at the chance to get out of here and return to what he had known before, but with Bailey standing in front of him, it didn't seem as pressing as it once had. Maybe it was her he had been missing, not the life he'd lived when they were working together.

"Well then, I'm happy for you" she replied. "If it works, it works."

It was about the first nice thing she had said to him without any qualification, and he appreciated it. It felt as though they were finally starting to come to a place of understanding. Maybe they could even work together in taking out the men who had done this to her—to them. When he thought of how they had turned on her, his blood boiled, and he knew he needed to pull himself together before he made any kind of move. If he went after them now, he wouldn't have been able to contain his emotions. Bringing them down would need the kind of cool, levelheaded planning he wasn't capable of when he thought of her being hurt.

She brushed a hand over Wheatie's nose again, and the horse snorted happily before she turned and trotted back into the field to graze. Bailey's gaze lingered on her for a moment, a small smile on her face. Aaron just stood and looked at her. Being this close to her again, having her with him, was still surreal. He had never thought he would see her again, let alone in these circumstances, but he was glad he'd had the chance. If only so he could take the opportunity to clear the air a little about what had happened between them. He hadn't betrayed her—he'd only done what he needed to keep her safe, and he had to make sure she understood that.

"I'm going back up to the cafeteria for some food," she said finally. "You want to come with me?"

It was the first time she had actually offered to spend time with him by choice—a good sign.

Aaron nodded at once. "Yeah, sure," he agreed. "You need a hand getting down there?"

"I can walk, Aaron," she replied bluntly. "It just hurts a little. I'm not an invalid."

"Point taken," he replied, holding his hands up. "Anyway, I've been working all day. I'm starving. Let's go get some food."

The two of them made their way back to the main building together, talking easily about his work at Warrior Peak. He told her about the outbuildings, about bringing in the horses. It was just like old times. He was amazed at how easily they slipped back into their old dynamic, like they had never been apart.

The sky was clear and the sun was shining bright. It was the kind of strikingly beautiful day that Aaron had come to look forward to here. It was hard to believe that there was still so much danger and drama hunting them, everything he thought he had left behind all those years ago.

But for now, as he and Bailey made their way back toward the lodge, he didn't want to dwell on all of that. No, all he could think about was how good it felt to have her right there next to him again. The woman he hadn't been able to get out of his head, finally back by his side.

It felt right. Even if the circumstances were far from ideal.

Chapter Nine

Bailey woke with a start, her heart pounding and her eyes wide as she sat up straight in bed. The dream that had just plagued her was still fresh in her mind. She could almost see them crowding around her, the four of them staring down at her, not knowing if she was going to be able to get away. The flash of the knife had played in her mind's eye, the shock and fear of it. She had closed her eyes, ready for the end, only to open them again back in her temporary bedroom in Warrior Peak, right where she had fallen asleep.

She rubbed her eyes and planted her feet on the ground, doing her best to pull herself back together. It had been nearly three weeks since the attack, and she had been having nightmares about it nearly every night since. When were they going to go away?

When she put those guys behind bars where they belonged. That was when the nightmares were going to stop. After just over two weeks here, she was still no closer to actually tracking them down and exposing them for what they had done, and it was driving her crazy. She couldn't just sit around doing nothing. Yes, she was healing, but her mind was a mess, and she didn't know how to sort through everything going on inside of it.

She got to her feet and wandered out of the small room that had been assigned to her—nothing special, but it did the job. She was just glad to have somewhere to stay where she didn't have to be looking over her shoulder the entire time. This place was hardly ideal, though. She was surrounded by people she didn't know, still trying to figure out how many of them she could trust. But it was a place for her to rest, recuperate, and get back to full strength again.

Plus, Aaron was here, and they seemed to have finally started breaking down some of the barriers between them. There was so much history there that she knew it would be a while before they were anywhere close to normal, but she could work with that. At least he seemed willing to help her out with the crooked cops after them, if only to keep her out of trouble. She would take that.

She knew she could handle it all by herself if she needed to, but she was glad to have Aaron's help. She padded quietly along the corridors, toward the common room, where she knew there was a computer. She wouldn't be able to get back to sleep after that nightmare, and she needed something to keep her mind occupied until she could have breakfast. She had never been much of a morning person, but it turned out all it took was a terrifying encounter where she feared for her life to get her ass up and out of bed first thing. Who'd have thought?

She took her seat at the computer, which was set aside for residents to check emails and make video calls. It wasn't exactly high-tech, but she didn't need it to be. She just needed it to work. Before getting started with her search on Ziegler and the rest of the group, she sent her captain a message checking in and stating she needed a little more time before she returned to work. She had originally contacted him upon arrival after getting settled, feigning an unexpected emergency. He'd always been kind to her and agreed to her request as long as she kept him updated.

Once that was completed, she started to search for any information she could about Ziegler and his friends—anything at all that might hint someone else knew what she did. It was a long shot, but there had to be *something* out there. A mention in an article, an old report filed about them, any halfway coherent explanation as to how they had managed to get away with what they had for so long.

Nothing. There was nothing. She tried every search term she could, every approach she could think of, tapping in to every database she could imagine, but she couldn't find anything. An hour passed, and she gnawed on the inside of her mouth, trying to figure out the best way to get to the bottom of this.

What she really needed was interdepartmental information. Any notices that might have been passed back and forth between cops about what they were doing. She wouldn't be able to access them without arousing suspicion or even drawing attention back to Warrior Peak. Aside from the fact that'd be dangerous and risky, she didn't want to expose the people here like that. This was a sanctuary, a safe place for healing, and these people were kind and helpful. They didn't deserve that type of evil brought to their door. But if she could find someone who was already working within a department in some official capacity, who wouldn't look too strange delving into this stuff, it would be a start.

Maybe someone nearby? She started searching for sheriffs in the local area, trying to use her intuition to find one who looked trustworthy. Though, after what she had found out about the men she worked with, maybe she shouldn't trust herself on that front.

Eventually, she stumbled across the smiling image of a sheriff for the small town nearby. He was a little older, and his bio said that he had been serving the same small community for his entire career—over twenty years. Was that a good sign? It meant he had either earned the trust of the people around him, or he'd hung on to his position through more nefarious means. She wasn't sure. She would have to ask Aaron about it. He knew more about this place than she did.

All at once, she looked up and realized that sunlight had started to filter through the window in front of her. She had been so lost in her research, she had almost forgotten that there was still a day ahead of her. A few people were moving around upstairs, and she could hear one of the cooks humming to themselves as they passed by the common room on the way to the kitchen.

She quickly deleted her search terms and turned off the computer. For some reason, she didn't like the idea of anyone seeing what she had been looking for. Better to keep it to herself for now, until she was sure she could trust everyone around here.

She felt a little guilty for even thinking about them like that, when everyone had been nothing but kind and welcoming to her. By the sounds of it, everyone here had a story of their own, some of them probably a whole lot wilder than hers. Maybe she would get around to hearing them one day, once she had dealt with this mess of corrupt cops.

"Hey."

She whipped her head around as though she had been caught doing something she shouldn't. Cade stood in the doorway smiling at her, and she smiled back. Seeing him made her wonder if River was already around. She hadn't seen her in a few days and should probably touch base with her soon. River'd asked her to keep her updated on her therapy with Carter, and she needed to do that before she came looking for her on her own.

"Hi," she replied, her cheeks turning red. She didn't even know why.

"I see you're up early," he remarked. "I could use some help in the kitchen, if you're up for it."

She parted her lips, about to turn him down, but then she stopped herself. Everyone around here worked to keep the place running, and it would have been pretty rude if she'd just expected not to have to pull her weight.

"Sure," she replied.

He grinned. "Thanks."

"Is River up yet?" she asked as she looked around him. "I've been meaning to check in with her."

"Yeah, she's still at the cabin. She'll be down in a bit. Ready?"

"Yep. Put me to work." As she got to her feet and headed over to join him, he eyed her thoughtfully.

"What is it?" she asked, a little more defensive than she had intended to be.

"I just know that if you're up early, chances are it's not just because you're a morning person," he replied. "People get restless here. And I know a restless spirit when I see one. Come on, you're on bacon duty."

She followed him down to the kitchen, hoping he wasn't going to ask her anything too invasive about what brought her to Warrior Peak. Thankfully, he didn't seem interested in much more than setting her to work. As he chopped vegetables, he got her to man the stove, cooking pancakes and bacon until there was a heaping pile of them on the plate ready to be taken out to everyone.

"You've got a mean pancake-flipping arm," he remarked.

She laughed. "Hey, I guess you're never too old to learn new tricks, right?" she replied. She felt comfortable in his presence, which surprised her. She had been a little nervous around new men after what had happened, but Cade seemed to know not to go delving into her past. He had probably dealt with plenty of people like her over his time here, and the practice was obviously paying off.

"Okay, let's start plating up," he told her as people started to file into the cafeteria. The place was starting to fill with a warm chatter, and Bailey felt a million times more relaxed than she had when she had woken up. That seemed to be the magic of this place: It was meant to be a safe place for those who had nowhere else to go. Even though she had already stayed longer than she intended, she was glad to be here.

They began to carry the food out into the communal area, and she spotted Aaron sitting at the far end of one of the long tables. He grinned up at her when he saw that she had been put to work, and she couldn't help but smile back. God, it was still so strange to see him again, but she was glad to have a friendly face staring up at her among this sea of people she didn't know.

Once they had set out the food for everyone, she took a seat next to Aaron. Her mouth was watering now—all this cooking for other people had made her hungry. She hadn't been eating a whole lot since she'd gotten there, not wanting to take advantage of their generosity too much, but she tucked into breakfast like a starved animal.

"It's good to see you eating," Aaron murmured to her.

She glanced up, her heart flipping when she caught his eye. She couldn't stop thinking about what he had said to her the other day, when they had been out at the paddock together—that all he had wanted when he was back in Kings Mountain was her. If she had known back then that he felt that way, would it have changed things? Would she have made a move, or would she have forced herself to hold back because he was her superior? She didn't know.

"I've been up for hours," she replied through a mouthful of food. "Been looking into...well, you know."

He nodded.

"You should give yourself some time to heal," he reminded her gently. She knew he was just trying to help, but he must have been aware that she wasn't going to let go of it that easily. Maybe she could find some middle ground, instead of trying to shut him down again. They weren't going to make any progress if everything ended in a battle.

"Maybe we could go out to the paddock again today," she replied. "I'd like to see how Wheatie is doing."

"I'm sure she would be happy to see you," he told her, and she grinned.

She loved that horse. Heck, maybe she was starting to like it here more than she cared to admit. She never would have imagined she would feel safe anywhere after what had happened to her back in Kings Mountain, but she felt more comfortable in this place with each passing day.

As though he could see what was going on inside her head, Aaron leaned forward and lowered his voice. "See? It's not too bad here, once you get settled."

"Eat your breakfast," she said on a laugh, but he was right. This place had a lot to offer—and the longer she stayed here, the more she saw that.

Chapter Ten

As Aaron set about working on the cabin, he whistled through his teeth. Breakfast with Bailey was about the best way he could think of to start the day. Spending time with her stirred something inside of him he thought was gone for good. The reminder of how good it felt to be around her was bringing all sorts of emotions back to the surface. Feelings he'd pushed down long ago.

Plus, she seemed to be settling in a little better now, which made him happy. He was glad she was starting to see how good this place could be for her, especially after what she had been through. Nobody deserved to be assaulted the way she had been, but at least this was a safe space, somewhere she could heal and relax.

Even if she didn't seem very good at relaxing. She had never been good at it, actually—even when they worked together, she had always been looking ahead to the next case before the last one was even finished. It was something he used to tease her about, and she had always rolled her eyes good-naturedly and reminded him she was trying to make a name for herself.

But now? Now, things were different. This was about taking down the corrupt cops who had infected the department, not just handling a case. She would be even more laser focused on her goal than before, and he couldn't even imagine what that was going to look like.

He heard footsteps crunching on the grass behind him, and glanced around to see Bailey approaching. She was still limping slightly, but not as badly as she had been a week ago. She was healing fast, like her body was trying to prepare her for what lay ahead.

"Hey," he greeted her, straightening up.

"Hey," she replied. "What are you working on?"

"This old cabin needs some TLC," he remarked, nodding to the slightly dilapidated shack next to him. "I think it could make a good living space for someone once I've had some time to put it all back together again."

"Sounds like a heck of a job," she replied.

"It will be," he agreed. "But it's satisfying to see it all come together when it's finished."

She smiled but he could tell at once there was something on her mind. You didn't work with someone as closely as they had and not have an idea of what was going on inside their head.

"What's up?" he asked.

"Sheriff Willis," she replied. "You know him?"

"Yeah, he's the sheriff for the small town down the mountain," he told her, propping up his tools and turning to face her properly. "What about him?"

"You think he's trustworthy?" she pressed.

Frowning, he nodded. "He's never given me any reason to think he isn't," he replied. "Why do you ask?"

"I think he could be the contact I need in the force to dig up the information on Ziegler and his crew," she explained. "I can't use my own credentials—that'll make it easier for them to find me. But someone like him, he could."

Aaron sighed, leaning up against the shack. "You're not going to let this go, are you?"

"Of course I'm not," she replied, and she turned to head back toward the main building.

He took off after her. She was so focused on what she felt like she needed to do, she was going to walk herself straight into trouble if she wasn't careful. He knew he wouldn't forgive himself if something happened to her. She had already been through so much, and he wasn't about to let her walk into this mess without trying to deter her.

"Bailey, you don't want to start this fight," he warned as he matched pace with her.

She shot a look at him. "I'm not the one who started it, they are," she reminded him. "I'm just going to finish it."

She reached her truck and climbed in, wincing as she swung her leg in after her.

He stood in front of it, arms crossed. "I'm not going to let you go down there alone," he warned her.

She stared at him for a moment, as though daring him to try and stop her.

"You can either get out of my way, or you can help me," she replied. "Which one is it going to be?"

He paused for a moment, then let out a sigh, and gestured for her to get out of the truck. "Come on, let me drive," he told her. "Your leg's still healing."

She looked as though she was about to protest, but thought better of it. She climbed out and allowed him to take the driver's seat while she hobbled around and got in on the passenger's side. Being beside her again like this, it brought back a flood of memories. All those hours they had spent cruising around the county, talking, listening to music, and getting to know each other. In all the years he had been on the force, those had been his favorite memories.

Maybe he would be able to make some new ones with her before this latest mission was over.

They drove into town, and Bailey peered around, taking the place in with her incisive gaze. She had always been really observant, able to pick up on details that went over his head. It was one of the many things that would have made her an amazing detective, though he supposed he had shot her in the foot when he had written that report about her. He tried not to linger on the thought of it. He had done what he had to do at the time, and at least she was willing to let him help now, right?

They arrived outside the sheriff's station, and he helped Bailey out of the truck. Aaron didn't know Sheriff Willis particularly well, but he had met him a few times and the sheriff had always seemed capable and trustworthy. Reminded him of some of the cops he'd known when he was first starting out: Dedicated, focused, and committed to keeping the small town where he served a safe place for everyone.

Bailey led the way inside, where they found Willis leaning up against the reception desk. She smiled pleasantly at him.

He looked her up and down and extended his hand. "You must be new," he remarked. Aaron guessed he knew almost everyone in this town, which would make his job a lot easier.

Bailey took his hand, and nodded. She introduced herself. "I'm Bailey Masters. Nice to meet you."

"You too," Willis replied, and he nodded in greeting to Aaron.

"Sheriff Willis." Aaron returned the nod.

"So, what brings you in here today?" Willis asked, escorting them back to his office. "Nothing serious, I hope."

She grimaced. "I wish I didn't have to bring this to you, but I can't think of anyone else who can help," she explained. "Aaron told me you're a good cop, and we need more of those around. I'm really hoping you can help me out here."

She filled him in as quickly as she could on what had happened with the guys at Kings Mountain, and Willis paused to take it in, his eyes widening as the enormity of it seemed to settle over him. Though he had dealt with some big cases in his time, he had probably never had to work one that was aimed at his fellow cops.

"I'm so sorry that happened to you," he told Bailey, his voice quiet, as though he couldn't believe what he was hearing. "To think of our own people turning on us like that." He shuddered, shaking his head.

"It was an eye-opener for me, that's for sure." She nodded with a grim smile. "I never expected something like that from the guys I worked with."

"It's unthinkable," he muttered. "But I'm sure you understand where I'm coming from when I say I need a little more proof of your status. Do you have ID on you? Someone who can vouch for you?"

"Of course," Bailey replied, not missing a beat. She didn't seem offended at all. Aaron guessed she was just glad someone was actually listening to her and taking her seriously. She reached into her pocket and pulled out her ID, then handed it over. Willis inspected it for a moment, lifting it so he could compare the picture to her face. Satisfied, he nodded, and handed it back to her.

"Well, I hope I can be a better cop to you than those guys were," Willis remarked. "What exactly is it you need?"

"I need to get any information that has been passed around about them, what they've been doing, all of it," she replied. "There has to be someone who knows something and kept quiet, or someone who's passed something around the local departments, even if it's not much. I don't want to arouse any suspicion by going after it myself, but someone like you…they're far more likely to hand over what we need."

He nodded, leaning back against the desk.

"I'm not sure how much I'll be able to get," he warned her. "I'll look into what I can, but I don't know how much would have filtered down from Kings Mountain to here. I do have a few contacts around the state. They might be able to help out."

"Can you trust them?" Bailey asked.

Willis narrowed his eyes and nodded. "I'd trust them with my life," he replied firmly. "I'm happy to let you into the system, Bailey, but Aaron, you're not a cop, so I'm going to have to keep it in the business."

Bailey passed him a quizzical look. "Oh, but Aaron—"

"Of course, Sheriff," Aaron replied, cutting her off. He had never mentioned to Willis that he'd been a cop before, because he was worried it would bring up too much of his past that he didn't want to talk about. But the more he got to know the older man, the more he trusted him. Maybe he would start to come clean about some of his past when all of this was over.

If they could finish it, of course.

"But you might be better off talking to Lawson and Xavier about this," he continued. "They used to be CIA, after all."

Bailey spun around to face Aaron, her eyes wide.

"They *what*?" she demanded. "You never thought to tell me that?"

Aaron shrugged. He had his reasons. But he got the feeling he wasn't going to be able to keep them to himself for much longer.

Mainly because Bailey got the truth out of him, one way or another. He couldn't hide himself from her.

Even if that made him feel vulnerable in a way he hadn't for a very long time.

Chapter Eleven

"You think it's safe for us to be out like this?" Bailey whispered to Aaron, as they pulled the truck up to a restaurant at the edge of town.

He smiled at her, raising his eyebrows. "You have nothing to worry about," he promised. "It's just a little family-owned place. They don't ask any questions, apart from what kind of wine you want with dinner."

A smile spread over her face. "That sounds really good," she agreed, biting her lip excitedly.

Bailey and Aaron had spent the better part of the day with Willis, talking over everything that had happened and figuring out what their next moves were going to be. There was still a whole lot Willis needed to look into, and the best thing they could do for now was give him his space, and try to get some rest. Not that Bailey had been able to rest much, but he had convinced her to stop by this little Italian place on the edge of town before they headed home. The food was good at the lodge, but sometimes it was nice to get out and go somewhere fresh, especially when that place made the best garlic bread in the state.

Was this a date? She certainly wasn't trying to think of it like that. It was just a couple of old friends hanging out together, taking a chance to catch a breath after everything that had been going on. She might even consider him a friend again—or at least an ally. Yes, their past was messy, but they were working toward the same goal here, and that had to count for something.

The restaurant was quiet when they walked in, and they were led to a red-and-white-checked table at the far side of the room, next to the window. Trees swayed in the breeze beyond as the sun dipped behind the mountains. A single candle flickered between them. If it wasn't for the history between them, she would have said it was almost romantic.

"Why didn't you tell me about Lawson and Xavier being former CIA?" she asked as soon as they sat. Now that they were out of the sheriff's office and alone, she couldn't stop herself from interrogating him. She'd never been a patient person.

He shrugged. "I don't know much about it really. I do know that he and Lawson were in the military together," he admitted.

"You don't know much about it?" she replied, confused. "You've been living there for years now, right? It's never come up?"

"I guess I'm a bit of an outsider at the sanctuary," he explained. "I think it's because I kept to myself so much when I first arrived. I hoped that if I didn't ask people questions, they wouldn't ask me questions I didn't want to answer. I'm just the guy who fixes stuff, and I like it that way."

Her eyebrows drew together. "That's a shame," she remarked. "You think you could ask them about it? See if there's anything they'd be willing to do to help us?"

"Yeah, I think I could manage that," he replied. "I don't know them super well, but they don't like it when people are up to no good. There was some stuff that happened not too long ago with a gang that the sheriff asked for their help with. And if it's something that could possibly pose a threat to Warrior Peak, they'd definitely want to help."

"Hope so," she replied, as the waiter arrived with their menus. She turned her attention to the food options, and her stomach grumbled. She hadn't eaten since breakfast, too caught up with how much she felt like she had to do. She knew she needed to focus on taking care of herself, but at least Aaron was there to remind her to rest and eat.

"What's good here?" she asked, and he grinned.

"The garlic bread is amazing," he replied. "They make it fresh in-house. You have to try it."

"That sounds really good," she murmured, and her mouth started to water as some of the delicious savory scents came floating out of the kitchen. She began to relax as she cast her gaze over the menu, deciding what she was going to have. Her stomach had been in such knots when she'd first gotten here that she'd hardly been able to think about eating—now it was catching up with her.

They ordered a huge pile of food, until the table was practically quaking under the weight of it. She grabbed a slice of garlic bread first.

"Oh, my God, this garlic bread really is amazing," she hummed, as she took a bite of the cheesy, crispy, garlicky deliciousness that had just arrived.

He grinned at her. "See? I told you."

"I'll never doubt your opinions on Italian food again," she promised him. "You have my word."

Maybe it was the food, maybe it was the peace of the restaurant, or maybe it was finally getting a start on her mission, but she was really starting to relax now. They chatted about the sanctuary and about the small town they were in, Blue Ridge. It reminded her a little of Kings Mountain, except without the stress that was now tied to that place for her. She was amazed at how easily the conversation seemed to flow between them now that she was starting to let her guard down.

"You ever think about going back to being a cop?" she asked him with interest once they were waiting for their dessert.

He thought about the question for a moment, and then shrugged. "Sometimes," he admitted. "There's so much that's happened, I'm not even sure where I would be able to start. And I'd have to explain why I just walked away from it all those years ago."

"When people find out what kind of trouble you were in, they'll understand," she replied, catching herself off guard with how much she meant it. She'd had a hard time forgiving him for what had happened all those years ago, but knowing what she did now, she could better understand his reasoning.

"Plus, someone needs to bully the rookies until they harden up," she joked.

He laughed. "Hey, now, I was never a bully," he protested, shaking his head. "I just made sure they didn't get soft once they'd graduated training."

"Oh, yeah?" she fired back playfully. "And when you used to call them on the radio and send them to the middle of nowhere, that was part of hardening them up too, was it?"

"You were just as guilty of that as I was," he reminded her, and she laughed as their order of homemade tiramisu arrived.

She could still remember the way they practically rolled around the car laughing together when they played these little pranks on the rookies in the department. They were probably a little mean, but when they were in it together, it didn't feel that way.

"Yeah, and you were my superior," she shot back. "So you're the one who'd have to answer for it. You were supposed to set a good example."

"I think I was setting a great example," he argued playfully. "Showing you how to let loose and have some fun for a change."

"For a change?" she protested, laughing. "You saying that I'm not fun?"

"I'm saying you were a rookie who took the work dead seriously," he replied, digging his spoon into their dessert. "And maybe you could use a little loosening up from time to time."

She stuck her tongue out at him, and he chuckled. She had always liked his laugh, how genuine it sounded, like he really meant it. There were so many guys who came across as so insincere—she had been on enough crappy first dates to confirm that theory—but he had never seemed that way to her.

It was starting to feel distinctly like old times, much to her surprise. When she had imagined seeing him again, she had never thought they would be able to talk like this. She had thought about chewing him out, giving him a piece of her mind, telling him off for what he had done to her, but never that they could sit around and laugh and talk about the past together, as though they were old friends.

As he looked at her, she felt the familiar flutter in her chest she had come to recognize when she was near him. And she knew that, no matter how much she might have wanted to tell herself otherwise, there was always something more than friendship between them.

"I guess we should be getting back to Warrior Peak," he remarked, once the waiter had cleared away the delicious tiramisu they'd shared.

"I'm not sure I can even walk, I'm so full," she groaned. "You're going to have to roll me back to the truck."

"Fine, as long as I'm driving," he replied.

"I can drive us back," she protested, but he held up the keys and raised his eyebrows at her.

"You're going to have to fight me for them."

He settled the bill, insisting on paying for it himself, and then they headed to her truck outside. She hadn't actually expected him to make her fight for her keys, but when she went to take them out of his hands, he held them high up over his head.

"I told you, I'm not letting you drive," he reminded her.

Her mouth fell open in surprise. "Aaron, it's my truck!" she protested, but she couldn't help but giggle. There was something about him when he was goofing around like this that just made her happy. He was normally so serious, or he had been back when he'd been at the station, apart from pranking the rookies. Knowing she got to see this side of him, this side he didn't seem to let many other people see, sparked something inside of her.

She stood on her tiptoes to grab the keys, but he was so much taller than her he could easily hold them over her head. She swiped for them, but she couldn't quite reach.

"You're going to have to do better than that," he teased her.

"Hey, no fair!" she argued, still giggling. He was acting so ridiculous, it was hard not to. And there was a spark in his eyes that reminded her of the old days—the days she had thought they had long since lost—but here he was, standing in front of her, looking at her like nothing at all had changed.

"I'm injured, this is practically bullying!" she continued, reaching up again.

He jingled the keys just out of her reach. "I'm sure you can handle it," he replied. "Besides, you shouldn't be driving on your injured leg, you know that."

"I can manage it," she told him, and he switched the keys from one hand to another, making it even harder for her. She hobbled around him, but it was too late. He was moving too quick for her, and it was clear from the look on his face that he was enjoying her struggle.

Or maybe just enjoying how close the two of them were to each other right now. Finally, he had lowered them just enough that with one more stretch she managed to lock her hands around the keys, and snatched them out of his grip.

"Got them!" she exclaimed, but as she lowered back down on to the balls of her feet, she was suddenly distinctly aware of how close the two of them were standing. Practically nose to nose, his eyes pinned to hers, the smile on his face shifting to something else as he looked at her. The warm light from the restaurant spilled out onto the sidewalk they stood on, the leaves blowing in the light breeze the only sound nearby.

She remembered, all at once, what he had said to her the other day, about how he had wanted her—and only her. Her old feelings, the ones she had tried to push down all this time, were starting to rise up again. She couldn't deny them any longer. He could feel the shift, too; she could tell by the look on his face as he stepped even closer. The chemistry was practically burning in the air between them, impossible to ignore.

He dropped his hand down to her face, and grazed his fingers along her chin, tilting her eyes up to meet his. Her heart hammered inside her chest as she looked up at him. How many times had she imagined exactly this? How many times had she longed for him to look at her the way he looked at her now? She couldn't count. But it was real, it was happening.

His eyes softened as he gazed at her, like it was the first time he had ever seen her. "You look so beautiful right now," he murmured.

Her breath hitched in her throat.

"I'm so sorry for everything, Bailey," he told her. "I never thought I was going to see you again, but I... I never stopped thinking about you. Not once. And I'm so glad you found your way back to me."

"Shut up," she said, a smile turning up her lips. "And just kiss me already."

And without any hesitation, he finally did.

Chapter Twelve

Aaron stared at the ceiling, listening to Bailey's breath settle back to normal again. A sheen of sweat on his brow spoke to the exertion they'd both just thrown themselves into. Even now, he could hardly believe it had happened.

From the moment their lips had touched back at the restaurant, he had known how he wanted this to end. He wanted to take her to bed, just like he had craved all those years ago. The desire and need were so strong he could hardly breathe, only this time, she wasn't his rookie. There was no reason to deny himself any longer.

They had driven back up to his cabin, his hand on her leg, the anticipation crackling in the air between them. How long had it been since they'd first met? And how hard had he worked to keep his feelings to himself? To finally do something about it felt electric, especially when he had never expected to see her again after what had happened between them.

They had stumbled through the door of his cabin and fallen into bed together, bringing to reality all the fantasies he'd had about her over the years. It had been so needy, so desperate, so full of all the built-up passion that they'd never been able to do anything about. It felt so damn right he couldn't believe it had taken them this long to finally make it happen.

He looked over at her, grinning, and she flashed him a smile. Her hair was a mess, her cheeks flushed, but she had never looked more beautiful to him.

"Good?" he asked her, reaching over to brush her hair away from her face.

"Oh my gosh, yes," she breathed, and she leaned over to plant a kiss on his lips. He couldn't get over how good they felt together, as though they had been made for each other. He knew he could never have done this when she was working as his rookie—it would have put both of their careers at risk. Besides, all that mattered was that they had this now. She was finally his, the woman he hadn't been able to stop thinking about, even after all these years.

She turned on her side and reached an arm over his chest, pressing her face against him and inhaling deeply, like she wanted to lose herself in his scent. He knew just how she felt. They had been apart for so long, it seemed as though they had so much catching up to do, so much of this passion to enjoy.

"I can't believe it took us so long to do this," she murmured, running her hand over his chest so she could feel the beating of his heart. He couldn't remember how long it had been since he'd been with someone—since before he came to Warrior Peak, at least—but he hadn't wanted anyone else, anyway. Only her.

"I know," he replied. "But you know the trouble it would have gotten us into if we'd done this before."

"Mmm," she agreed, and she closed her eyes for a moment. Of course, if they had done this before, he might not have been able to send her away when he needed to. It would have made his eventual betrayal of her—no matter how well-intentioned—hurt even more deeply than it already did. This was the right time for it, the time that made sense, and he was glad it hadn't happened before now.

"Yeah, everyone would have thought I was sleeping my way to the top," she remarked, grinning.

"Hey, if you're that good at it, it would probably have worked," he joked back.

She burst out laughing, burying her face into the pillow.

"Hey, glad you appreciate my skills," she said flirtatiously, turning to face him. A huge smile spread over her face as she looked at him, and he raised his eyebrows at her.

"What is it?" he asked.

"Nothing," she replied, shaking her head. "I just... I just thought about this a lot when we were first working together. I guess I had come to terms with it never actually happening, but...here we are."

"Here we are," he agreed, and he reached out to wrap his arms around her and pull her in close. Closing his eyes, he pressed his face into her hair, breathing in the scent of her deeply. Like her, he'd long since had to let go of the thought of something like this ever happening between them, but now it seemed like the most natural thing in the world.

He listened to the sound of her breathing as she began to doze off in his arms, and he just lay there for a while, enjoying the feeling of finally having her in his arms.

After all this time, they were both right where they needed to be.

He wasn't sure how long this newfound peace was going to last. But he would take as much of it as they could before their pasts caught up with them again. If anything, this was only going to bring them closer together, make it easier for them to work alongside each other once more.

His eyelids started to feel heavy as he drifted off to sleep. Contentment settled in for the first time in what felt like forever. All because of her.

Bailey.

Finally, they had cleared the air and were mending what he'd broken all those years ago. They had finally admitted their attraction to each other and were able to act on it.

They'd made their way back to each other, despite everything.

And now, they had to take on the corrupt cops who had driven them apart in the first place.

Chapter Thirteen

"Can you help me with these?" Hannah asked, holding up a bunch of flowers so big she could barely see out over the top of them.

Bailey couldn't help but smile at how ridiculous she looked, but she nodded at once.

"Of course I can," she replied, scooping a few of them from her hands. "Where are these going?"

"We're planting them up next to the paddock," she explained. "Aaron's done such great work there, and now that he's finished, we want to add a splash of color to finish it off."

"Sounds awesome," Bailey replied, perking up as soon as she realized it meant she was going to be able to see Wheatie again. And maybe Aaron, too. It had been only a couple of days since their night together, and she hadn't been able to stop thinking about him. But it wasn't the same confusing mess of emotions she was used to dealing with when it came to him. Instead, it was excitement, the thrill of a new romance, and the incredible heat of their chemistry.

She and Hannah headed out toward the paddock, where the sun was beating down on the fresh green grass sprouting up around the new fences Aaron had put up.

They both kneeled down at one corner, laying out the freshly uprooted flowers, ready to replant them—or they would have been, had it not been for Wheatie cantering over to see what they were doing.

"Wheatie, no!" Bailey exclaimed as the horse dipped her head down to take a chomp out of one of the flowers. She chewed thoughtfully for a moment, as though trying to decide whether she liked them or not, and then dived in to take a few bites out of the rest.

"Shoo! Shoo!" Hannah yelled, waving her hands at Wheatie to try and chase her away. But it was no good—the horse had already decimated at least half of the flowers.

"Wheatie, go away!" Bailey told her, but she couldn't help but laugh at how ridiculous this situation was. Wheatie could fit her head easily through the fence, and as soon as she had laid eyes on the flowers, she had seen her lunch.

"Look, I'll try to lead her away," Bailey told Hannah, and she scrambled over the fence, trying to gently direct the horse out of the chaos she was currently causing, but Wheatie just politely brushed her off, as though she was nothing more than an annoyance. Hannah burst out laughing, shaking her head.

"I think it's a lost cause," she told Bailey. "Don't worry about it, we can get more flowers. We just need to have a better defense system against Wheatie next time around."

"She's...a lot to handle." Bailey laughed, shaking her head. "Maybe we could ask Aaron to put up something, a blocker of some kind, just a temporary one to keep her out."

As though she had summoned him with just the power

of her words, she glanced around to see Aaron leaning on a shovel, watching the two of them. She felt a flush to her cheeks when she realized he had been staring, but she didn't mind.

"He's been watching you since you got out here, you know," Hannah said wryly.

Bailey raised her eyebrows. "Has he?"

"You didn't notice?"

"Nope," she replied, shaking her head. She felt like she would have been able to feel his eyes on her, but she had clearly been too distracted by Wheatie's mischief.

"Damn, girl." She laughed. "You should pay more attention when hot guys are checking you out."

"Hot guys?" she teased right back.

Hannah shrugged. "Hey, I'm not trying to jump in on your territory," she replied. "But he's cute. And it's clear he likes you."

Bailey shrugged. Aaron lifted a hand to wave at her, and she waved back. A flicker in her chest reminded her of just how attracted she was to this man. But she sure as hell wasn't going to go talking to Hannah about it. No, whatever was going on between them, it was just between them.

"The two of you have a history, right?" she pressed, her eyes widening with interest.

Bailey shrugged. "I guess," she replied, keeping it as vague as possible. Hannah was a really sweet woman, but it was going to take a long time for Bailey to totally trust anyone again.

Especially Aaron.

"Well, I think you should go for it," she told her, leaning forward and lowering her voice conspiratorially. "You don't want to leave him single for too long."

"Has he been dating other women? Since he got here, I mean?" she asked, hoping her voice was convincingly unbothered.

"Not that I've ever seen," Hannah remarked. "He's mostly kept to himself, actually. Nobody really knows a lot about what was going on with him before he got here."

Bailey watched Aaron as he headed back inside one of the sheds to finish his work. That made sense. It would explain why he didn't know a huge amount about Xavier or Lawson, even after living on the property and working here for as long as he had. She felt a little pang when she thought about that—that he had been holding back so much about himself, probably worried it was going to put either him or her in danger. No matter what he had done to her, he didn't deserve to live looking over his shoulder every moment, unable to be honest with anyone.

"Right," she replied.

"But you guys…it's clear there's something going on," she continued.

"Why do you think that?" Bailey replied.

Was it really that obvious to everyone else? She had hoped she might be able to keep it under wraps, at least for a little while, but it looked like the secret was out.

"Because he's always hanging around," she replied, nodding over to where Aaron had just been standing. "Come on, you must have noticed it, too. He used to hide out in his cabin most of the time unless he was working, and we would just see him at meals. But I feel like whenever I'm with you, he's there, too."

"Maybe," Bailey replied, but she couldn't help but

smile. Aaron had been looking out for her—just like he had done when she was a rookie. There was still so much of that dynamic between them, even if it had been twisted and nearly destroyed by what he'd done to her.

"He *likes* you," Hannah told her, and Bailey couldn't help but laugh.

"I'm not sure about that."

"Well, I am, and I'm never wrong about these things," Hannah replied matter-of-factly, and her confidence made Bailey giggle again.

Or perhaps it was just the thought of Aaron really liking her that had her all kinds of excited. She didn't know for sure what was going on between them right now, but she knew the night they'd spent together had been amazing.

"Aaron's a good man with a good heart," Hannah continued. "I don't know what happened between the two of you, but whatever it was, you shouldn't let it get in the way of whatever you feel for him now."

Bailey didn't reply, chewing her lip as she gathered what remained of the flowers before Wheatie made her way through them, too.

Hannah and Bailey headed back to the main building. Much to Bailey's relief, Hannah dropped the conversation about Aaron. Bailey wasn't sure how much longer she would have been able to throw Hannah off the scent, and the other woman didn't seem like she was good at keeping her mouth shut. Bailey could imagine her spilling the secret before she was ready, and it was hard enough to settle into this place without people wondering what was going on between the two of them.

Back inside the lodge, Bailey headed in for a quick

shower. There was dirt all over her from the flowers, and she needed to clean herself off before she helped out with anything else. More importantly, she needed a minute to herself, because she was starting to feel all kinds of flustered about what was going on with her and Aaron.

She closed her eyes as she stepped beneath the rush of the warm water, letting out a breath she didn't even realize she had been holding. Her mind drifted back to their first kiss. The feel of his fingers skimming across her skin, the way he looked at her, the way he spoke to her like she meant so much to him.

She had craved that from him for so long. Craved his touch, craved his approval, craved those precious words he had spoken to her. But it was all so wrapped up in their messy past, she wasn't sure how she was supposed to make it out the other side in one piece. Could she really forgive him? He had sent her away, and he had left those corrupt cops in the department without telling anyone. Even if he had had his reasons, even if it had been to protect her, it still didn't seem right.

But if she could end this—if she could expose those men, and bring a close to their reign of terror over that department—the past wouldn't be such a problem any longer. The problem right now was that they were still out there, and the danger was hot on their heels. Neither of them could relax and focus on the moment.

Well, maybe once. When they were lying in bed together the other night, she'd looked over at him and it had been like she was seeing him with clear eyes for the very first time. Like all their history had just vanished, and all that mattered was the man lying beside her—the man gazing at her like she was the most beautiful thing in the world. She couldn't think of anything that mattered more than the feeling in her heart right then, the warmth of it flooding her whole body.

She sighed as she stepped out of the shower. She wished she could go back to that moment, just for a second, just to feel the way she had felt then. One day, she would be able to. But for now? Until they could make their move on the dirty cops who had done this to them, they were stuck in this strange limbo, and she wasn't sure if she could handle it much longer.

Chapter Fourteen

"I think you should sit down," Xavier told Aaron, nodding to the seat on the other side of his desk. On either side of him, Cade and Lawson stood, flanking him like they were in formation.

"Yeah, thanks." Aaron sank into the seat and tried to gather himself. He had come here for a reason, and they were as aware of it as he was.

"So, what's going on? Why did you want to see all of us together?" Xavier asked, clasping his hands on the desk and giving him a serious look.

When Aaron had asked for a meeting with the other men earlier that day, he had known they could tell that something was up. He never tried to spend extra time with anyone here. Not that he didn't like them, but it just seemed safer to keep to himself.

But he needed their help. More importantly, so did Bailey. They had some serious skills if they were former military, then also adding Lawson and Xavier's former CIA experience. They could probably make good use of them in their quest to bring Ziegler and his crew to justice.

"I've been talking to Bailey," Aaron explained. "And

we…a lot went on in our past. I already filled you two in on some of it." He nodded between Lawson and Xavier, and then looked to Cade. "To keep it short and simple, Bailey and I worked together before. I was a police sergeant for a town similar to here in Blue Ridge, and Bailey was a rookie at the time—training under my supervision. We were in a small department with a handful or so of other guys. We handled mostly small-town stuff, nothing too serious for the most part, but we kept on top if it."

Lawson and Cade exchanged a glance when he paused.

Xavier nodded at him to go on. "And?"

Aaron filled them in on the rest of the story, how he had discovered some of them were corrupt, and they had beaten the hell out of him, and then threatened to come after Bailey if he didn't leave. The report he had written to get her removed, and the six years they had spent apart in the meantime. How she had come back, only to be faced with the same betrayal he'd been through all those years ago, and how she was determined to take them down.

The men fell silent for a moment when he was done, taking in the enormity of what he had just told them.

"That's why you've kept to yourself all these years." Cade hit the nail on the head with that one guess.

Aaron nodded in agreement. "I was really messed up from everything when I first got here, and just wanted to forget about it. Plus, I thought if I talked about it to anyone, I might end up drawing them to me somehow and something worse might happen. It just felt safer to stay out of the way and keep my head down."

"Now, I've heard a lot of stories from people who've

ended up here," Lawson remarked, finally. "But that has to be one of the wildest."

Xavier chuckled, and nodded in agreement. "Yeah, but that doesn't mean we can't help with it," he replied. "Bailey's been leading the charge so far, right?"

"Trying to…so far," Aaron replied. "I've tried to get her to slow down, but she wants to finish this."

"I can't say I blame her," Cade chimed in. "Sounds like she's committed her life to the force, so of course she wouldn't want to let that corruption go."

"Yeah, but I don't think it's a good idea for her to be involved in this anymore," Lawson added.

Aaron raised his eyebrows. "You don't?"

Good luck telling her that.

She had never been good at hearing *no*, especially when it was a case she felt personally connected to. And this one was about as personal as they came.

"She's got too much on the line not to get distracted," Xavier agreed. "And besides, if she does want to get back to work eventually, she's not going to want to have a history of working with people off the books."

Aaron grimaced. He hadn't even thought of that. Bailey was so focused on dealing with this in the immediate, she hadn't thought about how it might impact her career in the future. She had so much potential, even after being stuck behind a desk for so long, and he didn't want her to risk putting all of that on the line.

"You're right," he agreed.

"We need to get all the details she has to combine with yours, but I think it's best if we handle it from here on out," Xavier assured him. "And of course, we'll keep the two of you updated every step of the way. But it's better for her in the long term if she holds back from this."

"We can find somewhere else for her to stay so she's not tempted to get involved," Lawson added.

Aaron felt a twist in his chest at the thought. Losing her again, when she had only just come back into his life? It didn't feel right. But their help would be invaluable to bringing this to a close, and Bailey would surely recognize that.

He hoped, anyway. And he hoped her leaving wouldn't put an end to what the two of them had just started to share after all these years.

"Yeah, I agree with these two. It's too dangerous and could cause more problems down the line if she's involved in this. We'll come to her for information, if needed," Cade agreed. "But she can't be involved with the actual operation. I'm sure she'll be safer somewhere else, too."

"Yeah, apparently they know I'm here," Aaron admitted, and Xavier jerked his head back in surprise.

"You could have told us that sooner," he replied. "If they know you're here, there's every chance they know she's here, too. We'll need to lock down any information coming in and out, make sure we don't have any leaks."

"Agreed," Lawson replied. "Aaron, we'll get started on this today and start working out a plan. You can tell Bailey what's going on and we'll get with you both later to confirm information. We'll also find somewhere else for her to stay as soon as possible."

"I'll talk to her and fill her in," Aaron confirmed. But he had a bad feeling about this.

He had made a decision for Bailey before in the past, and he was pretty sure some part of her still hated him for it. He doubted she was going to take this well, no matter how sensible it was.

"Uh, one more thing, guys," he said hesitantly. He hoped what he was about to say wasn't going to have a negative impact on anything they'd be planning. "Bailey and I spoke with Sheriff Willis the other day in town, and she filled him in on some of it, hoping he could search for information for her."

The guys all exchanged glances, sharing unspoken words within those looks.

"We'll check in with Willis and see if he's made progress up to this point. Let him know we're on it now," Lawson told him.

"We'll talk to you later today," Xavier replied, rising to his feet and opening the door for Aaron. "And Aaron, thanks for coming to us with this. We haven't known a lot about you or your past up to this point. We didn't want to push and make you feel like you had to defend yourself to stay here. We wanted you to know you were welcome, regardless of your past. You know you can trust us, right?"

Aaron nodded. "I know. And I appreciate it. I should have made more of an effort before to open myself up and get to know all of you, but I was…scared, I guess. That I'd bring trouble if other people knew, and I just wanted to forget it all and disappear. And I thought I was doing right by Bailey at the time. I didn't have time to think it all through properly. I never expected her to come back after everything that happened." He paused, suddenly thinking his words were getting too heavy. "Anyway, thank you. For everything." He nodded at them all, then turned to leave.

He meant it. He knew he needed to start putting more trust in these guys. They had been there for him when he had needed it most, even if he hadn't told them the truth about what had brought him to Warrior Peak until now.

Now, he had to go tell Bailey the news. And he got a feeling she wasn't going to take it well.

It was another beautiful day outside, and Aaron knew exactly where Bailey would be—out at the paddock, hanging out with Wheatie. The bond she'd made with the old mare was downright adorable to him, bringing out this softer side of Bailey she didn't always show. He hoped she would be in a good mood when he got there, something to soften the blow of the news he was about to share with her.

He followed the path out to the paddock, and sure enough, she was standing with Hannah and River, the three of them laughing as they tried to shoo Wheatie away from the flowers they wanted to plant there. He paused for a moment, and couldn't help but smile.

She didn't see him yet, and the way she was interacting with the other women reminded him of how well she was settling in here. She might not have come to this place under the best of circumstances, but it was clear she really belonged. He had never really had much of a chance to see her outside of work before, and this relaxed version of Bailey was one he was really falling for.

Hannah glanced up and saw him standing there, and gave him a big wave. He lifted his hand to greet her, and Bailey looked up to see him, too. A small smile spread across her face, and his heart twisted hard in his chest. He hated that he was going to have to give her bad news, especially when it seemed like she was having such a good day.

He made his way toward them, his mind racing. Well, he couldn't tell her in front of the other women, that was for sure. Maybe that would give him some kind of an out? He didn't want to outright ask River and Hannah to leave—that would be rude of him. That would also invite all sorts of unwanted questions and probably hurt their feelings. And he didn't want to dampen the mood, since it looked like they were having so much fun. He would have to wait until the two of them were on their own.

He finally reached them, and Hannah tapped the fence beside her.

"You're going to have to come up with something better than this," she remarked playfully. "Wheatie and the other horses have been demolishing our flowers."

"Yeah, I think they've eaten a solid pound each." Bailey laughed, shaking her head. "I thought she was my friend, but Wheatie totally ignores me when the flowers are around. She's got a one-track mind!"

They all giggled, and Aaron grinned. How could he break this good mood with such bad news? He would wait a little while longer. He knew how badly he had let her down before, when he had written that report about her, and it felt like this would be an echo of that again. Sent away from the action, when she wanted to be in the middle of it.

"Maybe I can put something up so you can at least get them planted," he suggested, and he headed toward the shed where he kept his tools. A little guilt stirred in him as he thought about what he was hiding from her, but it was for the best.

At least, that was what he had to tell himself.

Chapter Fifteen

"If you hold the pallet up there...yes, that means she can't duck under it to get to the flowers."

Bailey instructed Aaron as Hannah and River went to work planting the flowers. Wheatie pawed at the ground, clearly a little annoyed that she couldn't get at her favorite snack.

Bailey reached out to pet her apologetically. "There's plenty of grass here for you, Wheatie," she reminded her. "You don't have to eat our flowers."

Aaron chuckled. "I'm not sure she's going to listen to reason," he warned her.

Bailey shrugged. "She deserves an explanation," she replied, smiling.

Today had been about as peaceful and perfect as she could imagine. She'd come out with Hannah and River first thing in the morning to get these flowers planted around the paddock. Now, Aaron was out with them, manhandling a pallet around to make sure the horses couldn't gobble them up before they were planted.

The sun was shining above them, and the horses were keeping them company, watching them as they tried to get their work done. Bailey was sure that they would descend on the newly planted flowers the first chance they got, but hopefully enough would survive to pollinate and actually get some color out in this part of the land. She could imagine how beautiful it was going to look in the summer, how striking and bright.

If she stuck around that long, of course. She had found herself thinking about the future here, which surprised her. It had been a last resort when she'd arrived, but as her body started to heal properly and her mind began to settle, she could see herself staying. It was like a little sanctuary away from the rest of the world. Even if she missed her work, she found purpose here, and it was a pleasant change of pace. This sure beat sitting behind a desk like she had been doing for all those years, anyway.

"I think that's the last one!" Hannah exclaimed as she got to her feet and dusted off her hands. Her knees were stained with grass and dirt, but she didn't seem to notice. Aaron lowered the pallet he held so he could see their hard work.

He nodded in approval. "Looks great."

As soon as he took his eye off the horse, Wheatie lunged forward again, but Bailey caught her before she could eat the flowers.

"Hey, you leave those alone," she scolded her playfully. "You've got to show some self-control, girl."

"I think I need to take a shower," River remarked, looking down at her grass-stained clothes. "Do you need a hand moving the pallets, Aaron?"

"No, I'll be fine," he replied as he hefted one up into his arms. The muscles in his biceps flexed slightly, and Bailey quickly averted her gaze. She was still getting used to seeing him out of his uniform, and she had to admit, there was something seriously sexy about him in a T-shirt and a pair of well-fitting jeans.

"I'll stick around and help," she offered without thinking.

Hannah shot her a look, and Bailey knew at once what was on her mind. She raised her eyebrows at her pointedly, as though daring her to say something, and Hannah grinned and followed River to the path back to the main lodge.

"You sure?" Aaron asked. "I can manage it myself—"

"You said you need to move them to the other shed, right?" she reminded him. "I can give you a hand with that."

"You sure you're feeling up to it?"

"Aaron, I'm fine," she told him. She knew he was just trying to look out for her, but she was really feeling so much better. Her leg still twinged every now and then, but the wound had healed well, thanks to the help of the women and the physical therapy.

"If you're sure," he replied, and they began to carry the empty pallets toward the outbuilding at the far corner of the paddock.

"I never tagged you for a horse girl," he remarked to her as they walked.

"I don't think I was," Bailey replied. "Until I met Wheatie, at least. She's just such a sweetheart. With the worst attitude ever."

Aaron laughed. "Yeah, I can see that," he agreed. "You think she's going to leave those flowers alone?"

"I think they're going to be gone before we even get back there," she replied as they carefully put down the pallets inside the other outbuilding. The shed still needed a lot of work done on it, but judging by the job Aaron had done on the other one, it wouldn't be an issue for him.

They turned to head back through the long grass around the paddock. The sun was just starting to dip a little lower in the sky, and a coolness had settled into the air. Their hands brushed against each other as they walked, and a jolt of electricity rushed from his fingertips to hers. She drew her hand away quickly. She still didn't know exactly where they stood, and she didn't want to confuse the matter any further.

Aaron cleared his throat. "I spoke to Xavier and Lawson today. And Cade, too. He's part of a tactical unit they train and run out of here."

Her eyebrows shot up excitedly. "You did? What did they say? Are they willing to help?"

"They are," he replied, but she sensed a hesitation in his voice that told her there was a *but* coming.

"Okay, good," she replied, frowning in confusion.

He sighed and looked down at her. "But they don't want you involved in the case any longer. They also want to move you to a safehouse while they get everything in order."

She stopped dead in her tracks. She must have heard him wrong. What was he talking about? She was the one who had been attacked by those guys! She was the only one who was still a cop, for God's sake! They couldn't expect her to just drop this, like it didn't matter to her.

"What did you just say?" she demanded.

He shook his head. "I'm sorry, I know it's not what you wanted to hear," he apologized.

She almost laughed at how ridiculous that statement was. Not something she wanted to hear? Yeah, you could say that again. She had been working behind a desk for so long to get where she was right now, only for him to turn around and tell her she couldn't be part of this mission? It was ridiculous.

"No way," she snapped at him. "No way. I'm not letting go of this. I'm the only one with the credentials—"

"Yeah, and that's exactly what they're worried about," he shot back. "They're worried that your involvement might put your future career at risk."

"And I won't even have a future career if these cops don't get what's coming to them!" she protested. "I can't... I can't believe you would do this to me. You really think this is a good idea?"

"I think you're great at your job, and you would be an asset to any team," he replied carefully. "But this is dangerous. And you don't want to put your future on the line when you have people who are willing to handle it for you."

"I don't want them to *handle* it for me," she replied through gritted teeth. "I want to handle it myself. I don't see what's so hard to understand about that."

They stared at each other for a moment, and she felt the anger crackling in her system. After everything they'd been through, he was doing this to her again. He was pushing her out of something that mattered to her.

"I don't want you to get hurt, Bailey," he told her, and she tore her gaze away from him. Was he right? Probably. But that didn't make this any less painful, didn't make listening to this any easier.

"And what about how I feel?" she demanded. "What about what you did to me? What you're doing to me right now?"

She took a step closer to him, her anger getting the better of her. He stood his ground. He wasn't going to budge on this, she could tell. He had made up his mind, and he had decided this was what was best for her. She couldn't believe it, couldn't wrap her head around him doing this to her again, as though they hadn't been through enough already. They had found each other again and she had finally started to trust him, and then this. This betrayal. Again.

"If you think I'm going to let you stop me—"

"If you think I'm going to let anything happen to you, you've got another thing coming," he replied.

Their hands grazed again, but this time, the electricity matched the anger in her body and morphed into something else entirely.

She pressed her lips to his before either of them could say anything else. She knew they weren't going to resolve this by talking, she knew she couldn't change his mind right now, and all she wanted was to find the one thing both of them could agree on. The feel of their bodies together, and the lure of this chemistry that never seemed to go away.

His hands tangled into her hair, and she kissed him hard, desperately—needing more, needing as much as she could have from him and so much more. His touch aroused her in a way nothing else did, and even though they were right out there in the middle of a field, she couldn't deny how much she wanted him.

Before she knew it, they were sinking down in the long grass together, and forgetting everything else but the intensity of this kiss.

Chapter Sixteen

"So, what have you got?" Aaron asked as he took his seat at Xavier's desk once more. This time, Lawson and Cade had pulled chairs around as well, a few pages of notes and screenshots lying out on the table in front of them. It was clear they had been hard at work, and Aaron appreciated the effort.

"I've been scouring the social media pages of everyone you mentioned to us," Xavier explained. "Most of them were smart enough to have everything on lockdown, but Benning was tagged in a few pictures with his ex-girlfriend. Looks like they were together until a few months ago and, judging by some of her posts after they broke up, it didn't exactly end well."

Aaron nodded. That made sense. It was hard to imagine someone like Benning in a good relationship—hell, any of them, really. With the subterfuge and lies they had to live their lives under, how could they ever really be honest with anyone?

"If we can get her to talk, we can find out what she knows about Benning and the others," Lawson added. "Seems like he'd be the kind of guy who'd have a hard time keeping his mouth shut, and he might have been flashing his cash with her in a way that made her suspicious. If we can get enough intel from her, it could be enough to get us a warrant and Bailey can take it from there."

"What are we waiting for, then?" Aaron asked as he pulled one of the screenshots on the desk toward him to take a look. Sure enough, there was Benning, his arm wrapped tight around a woman who looked more like she was grimacing than smiling. He couldn't help but feel sorry for her. She had been dating a cop, probably thought he would be the kind of stand-up guy she could trust, only to find out she had managed to land one of the worst of the bunch.

Xavier and Lawson exchanged a look.

"There's one problem," he replied. "It doesn't look like she's willing to...talk to any guys about this. Seems like the experience with Benning was enough to make her wary of men. Especially law enforcement types. So, we're going to have to find some other way to get to her."

Aaron leaned back in his seat, staring at the picture. He couldn't blame her for feeling that way. He had left his own life behind when he had found out the crap those men were tied up in. And being even closer to him? That would have screwed with her head in a big way.

But it posed a real problem. There was no way any of them could get her to talk without scaring her, and it was unlikely she would be willing to give them any useful information. They would need to find a woman to do it, but none of the women could know what was going on here. There was only one woman Aaron could think of who would fit the bill, but there was no way.

"I'll do it."

All four men looked up to see Bailey standing there,

her mouth set in a hard line, her eyes sharp as she glanced around the room at them. She must have been listening at the door. Aaron hadn't told her about this meeting, so he had no idea how she'd found out about it, but it was clear from the look on her face that she wasn't going to leave.

"Bailey, what are you doing here?" Xavier asked, sounding annoyed. "Aaron was supposed to tell you—"

"I did," Aaron fired back. Bailey narrowed her eyes at him. In all fairness, their conversation had been cut off before they could come to any conclusions about what they were going to do. As much as he wished he could have convinced her, as soon as she had planted her lips on his, he had known he was done for.

"You need a woman for this job," she replied. "I'm a woman. And I know what I'm doing. I know what we need to get out of her to get the warrant—"

"How long have you been listening in?" Lawson demanded, but she ignored him, not taking her eyes off Aaron.

"I can do this," she murmured to him, her voice almost pleading, as though she was begging him to see her as strong and capable. He felt a tug in his chest, but he pushed it down. He couldn't let his emotions get the better of him. He had just gotten her back, and he wasn't going to let her get hurt or mess up her future if he could help it.

"No," he replied, getting to his feet and shaking his head. "Sorry, Bailey, but no. We talked about this, and we decided it's not safe for you. You know why."

"And you know you can't do this without me!" she exclaimed. She was getting heated. Aaron should have known their encounter the day before wouldn't be enough to shut down her usual stubborn, focused self. When she got something into her head, nothing was going to stop her, especially a bunch of men telling her she couldn't do something.

"You're staying here, where it's safe," he replied. "They already know the lodge exists. At least that's a known fact."

"No, I'm not," she snapped back. "You can't just make these decisions for me, Aaron. I'm sick of it!"

Her words hung in the air, laced with more meaning than he cared to acknowledge. He knew he had to stop this. He didn't want Xavier and Lawson hearing all the ins and outs of their messy history, but there was nothing else he could do. She was going to make him have this argument right here, right now, in front of everyone.

Luckily, the guys seemed to realize this wasn't a conversation they should be sitting in on, and all of them made their excuses and hurried off. Bailey and Aaron were alone together again, but this time, there was none of the chemistry between them there normally was. No, it was just anger and all the feelings of hurt and betrayal.

"This is exactly what you did to me six years ago," she told him, tears rising in her voice. "I… I can't believe you think I would just go along with this again. Don't you know me at all?"

"I wanted to protect you," he replied through gritted teeth. "That's what I'm trying to do now. You know that, right?"

"You don't need to protect me," she shot back. "You didn't need to protect me then, and you don't need to protect me now—"

"Of course I needed to protect you back then!" he exploded at her. "They were going to hurt you, Bailey. You have no idea what they were capable of!"

"I know that they weren't capable of anything the two of us couldn't have handled together," she replied, her voice dropping. "You should have told me, Aaron. You know I would have helped you. Hell, I would have run with you, if you'd asked me to."

That stopped him dead in his tracks. He stared at her.

"You would have?" he murmured.

She nodded, her eyes dropping, a tear running down her cheek. "Of course I would have, Aaron," she told him. "I would have left with you. I was in love with you, I would have done anything you'd asked me to. *Anything.* As long as it meant we could be together. I would have chosen you over my career, my safety, anything. I just wanted you."

He couldn't bear to hear her say this. It hurt too much. If he could go back in time and tell this to his younger self, he would done things differently. He would have kept her close to him, supported her, maybe even worked with her to take them down.

But it was too late for that now. The damage was done. And he wasn't sure if there was anything he could do to put the pieces back together.

"I loved you, too, Bailey," he replied, his voice catching at the back of his throat. "That's why I did what I had to do. And that's why I'm doing this now. I can't live with the thought of you getting hurt because of me—not again."

He couldn't even finish what he was saying—the thought of it was far too painful. He couldn't bring himself to acknowledge the truth of what he had put her through, especially knowing how deeply she felt for him. It made him feel even guiltier, knowing how much he had hurt her without even realizing it. He hated himself for what he had done to her.

"That's not how love works, Aaron," she replied, shaking her head. "You don't take someone's choices away when you love them. You work with them. You talk to them. You tell them what's going on. You don't just throw them away."

He parted his lips to try and protest, but he couldn't think of anything to say. She turned away before he could speak, and headed for the door. When she got to the door, she paused for a second with her hand on the knob, like she might say something else, but instead she opened the door and left the room.

He listened to the sound of her footsteps down the corridor, the sound of her words ringing in his ears. She had loved him. She had loved him so much she would have given up everything to be with him. Instead, he had taken that choice from her. He had taken away everything she had worked for, everything she had dedicated herself to, and then left her alone, without the support of the man she had loved.

He felt like she had punched him in the stomach. This pain was worse than anything he'd ever felt before, worse than the beating he'd taken from Ziegler and his men. Because this was a pain he had inflicted on to her, a pain he would never be able to undo. The way she saw it, he was just doing the same thing he had done to her six years ago, and he couldn't even argue with her.

But he couldn't stand the thought of her out in the line of fire again. He wouldn't be able to live with himself if something happened to her, just like he couldn't have all those years ago. He could still remember when they had threatened her, when they had told him they would take her out if he didn't do what they said, and the sheer terror that had consumed him when he had been forced to confront the thought of losing her.

So much terror, he hadn't even thought about how she felt about all of it. He wished he could go after her, find the right thing to say to fix it, but the pain in her eyes when she looked at him ran deep. Maybe deeper than he would ever be able to reach.

He sank back down into the chair and let out a sigh. It was never easy with her. No matter what he did, no matter how he tried to look out for her, he always seemed to find some way to mess it up and hurt her in the process. How much longer was she going to let him keep doing this?

How much longer was she going to stay in his life?

Chapter Seventeen

As Bailey piled clothes into her bag, she dashed away the tears that had started to fall from her eyes. She didn't need to be emotional right now. There were more important things to deal with.

Like getting out of here.

She'd made the decision after her conversation with Aaron earlier in the day. She just couldn't stay at the sanctuary, not as long as he was there. She felt her old emotions rising up again, the attachment to him deepening faster than she could stop it, and she just couldn't let herself go through it all again.

He wanted to protect her, but what he didn't realize is that she didn't need him to fight her battles *for* her, she needed him to fight her battles *with* her. As much as she loved him, she couldn't be with someone who was going to make decisions for her and treat her like she wasn't capable. It broke her heart to leave so soon after they had found each other again and confessed their feelings, but she wouldn't stay to be treated like some damsel in distress.

She knew he had reasons for wanting her to sit this out and let him and the other men handle it, but it didn't feel good to be pushed out of a situation that was so important to her. And while she appreciated that he cared about her safety and her future career, she needed to be involved in taking these bad men down. She was the one who had nearly died at their hands, and she was expected to just...step aside, let someone else take care of it for her? No. That wasn't who she was. It wasn't who she had ever been, and she wasn't going to start now.

She'd seen the screenshots they'd had laid out on the desk, so at least she had something to work with. If they had been able to find this information on social media, there was a good chance she would be able to do the same thing. Once she figured out who this woman was, she could go talk to her and get any information she was willing to share. Hopefully, it would be enough to get a warrant.

And she could go back to the Bay, see if any of her friends there were willing to work with her. She had been too scared to even think of it before, but now it seemed like a pretty sensible idea. She could go to them, explain everything that had happened, and with the information she managed to glean from Benning's ex-girlfriend, they could make a move and end this corrupt circle for good.

Her mind had been racing all the way through dinner, where she had played nice with everyone, not wanting anyone to guess what was going on inside her head. She didn't want them to keep an extra watch on her. She was going to sneak out of there in the middle of the night, and then she could start out on her own again.

All on her own. A pang hit her chest hard, and she had to stop and take a deep breath to gather herself. How was she going to manage that? All alone? It just didn't seem fair or right. She had come here because she had wanted

Aaron's help, and while he had given it to her, it had been the same kind of betrayal he'd done before. Even if he had his reasons, and even if she understood them to some extent, she couldn't let him do this to her again.

Once she had gathered a few supplies, clothes, and some food she'd snuck from the kitchen, she opened her bedroom door as quietly as she could and stepped into the corridor. She shot a look one way and then the other, making sure nobody was out there. It was just past midnight, and the physical work everyone did during the day meant they slept pretty deep. There was no reason anyone would be up and about at this time of night.

Which meant there was nobody to stop her.

She started to creep down the corridor, and something at the back of her mind silently wished someone would catch her doing this. Then she could make her excuses and stay. They didn't want her to leave, and she knew she was going to miss so much about this place—the views, the horses, and the women she had grown friendly with.

And Aaron, of course. Mainly Aaron.

He was going to be devastated when he found out she was gone—she wouldn't be surprised if he tried to catch up with her and bring her back. She hoped that he would just let her leave. She didn't have the strength inside to hold off against her attraction to him, and if he came for her, she might just go back with him.

No. She had to be strong, she had to be sure of herself. She couldn't let these ridiculous doubts get caught up in her mind. She padded down the stairs and to the front desk, where she grabbed a set of truck keys hanging on a rack behind the counter for one of the older vehicles on the property. She felt bad for stealing from them when they had been so good to her, but she didn't want anyone to immediately realize she was gone and track her truck. And she knew Aaron would do it, too. He'd follow her and try to convince her to come back. Besides, she wouldn't keep theirs forever, she'd bring it back when she was through with it. Her own had sentimental value and she'd want it back eventually. Hopefully, no one here would hold the theft against her.

She just had to bring down the dirty cops, once and for all. And she would—with or without help. She'd show them all she was capable.

Outside, the night was still. The only sound was the grass rustling around her as she made her way up the main path that led from the central building. Her heart was in her throat as she quietly unlocked the truck door and climbed in. She couldn't believe she was doing this. A part of her was screaming to turn around and go back. She could go back upstairs, slip back into her bed, and act like this never happened. Wake up tomorrow, go down to breakfast just like usual...

No, she couldn't do that. She pushed the key into the ignition, her eyes blurry with tears. Gritting her teeth, she felt the engine come to life beneath her. Glancing over her shoulder to back up, she put the rusty old truck into motion, her first step on her journey out of here.

Then, something caught her eye. For a moment, she thought she had imagined it—a tiny movement at the very edge of her vision. If she hadn't been so hyperalert, she might not even have noticed it. But she looked around and saw some movement at the top of the path that led through the forest and into the paddock.

"What the hell?" she muttered to herself, and she

pushed the door open and slipped her feet back to the ground again.

It must have been an animal, something like that. She tried to soothe her panicking mind, and she was about to climb back into the truck to leave when a scent wafted by her on the wind. She sniffed the air. What was that?

Then her heart dropped. It was oil. That was the smell of oil.

Before she could react, the sky lit up in a flash of flames, and she could see the paddock in the distance bursting into a fireball. Her eyes widened, and she clapped a hand over her mouth. The horses had been moved to another paddock while the buildings were being finished up to be weathertight, but if that fire spread, it could easily reach them—or the main building, if it was left long enough.

"Fire!" she screamed at the top of her lungs. "Fire!"

She felt as though she was frozen to the spot, trapped exactly where she stood as she tried to pull herself together. She couldn't just walk away from this. Someone was targeting them, she was sure of it. The fire was spreading unnaturally fast, and whatever accelerant they had used was clearly working exactly as they had intended it to.

Bailey leaned on the truck's horn and yelled for help. Within a few minutes, the residents of the lodge were pouring out onto the grass around her. Cade shielded River from the sight, and she pressed her face into his chest as though she couldn't believe what she was seeing.

"Get as many buckets as you can from the supply closet!" Xavier yelled, springing into action. "Hannah, get a hose hooked up and call the fire department—come on, we need to move!"

Everyone was rushing around a moment later, trying to stop the fire before it got any worse, but Bailey just stood there. She wanted to help, she did, but she felt trapped. She needed to make sure Aaron was okay before she left while everyone else was distracted by the fire. What if he had been out working late at the shed and been caught in the blaze?

"Oh, God."

She heard a voice behind her, and spun around to see Aaron standing, ashen faced, a few feet away. He must have come from his cabin as soon as he heard the commotion. She breathed a sigh of relief as soon as she saw him, and she wanted to hug him, hold him, tell him how sorry she was. How she was sure this had something to do with her, his little piece of heaven torn apart by something he had tried to leave behind.

He rushed toward the rest of the group to help, but Bailey hesitated. Should she go after him? It was an all-hands-on-deck situation, that was for sure, and they would likely need all the help they could get.

But if she didn't leave now, she wasn't sure she would ever have the nerve to again. No, as awful as it was, she knew she couldn't stay here. She had to go. Guilt tore at her mind as she raced back to the truck, checking over her shoulder to make sure everyone was accounted for. She saw all the people who had helped her rushing to try and contain the fire. She wished them a silent goodbye, and a thank-you for everything they had done for her.

The tears flowed freely now as she reached the truck once more and climbed inside. Covering her face with her hands, she took a deep, shaky breath, trying to gather herself. She couldn't believe she was doing this when they were facing off against a ferocious fire, but she didn't have a choice. They couldn't help her. They wouldn't give her the justice she knew she needed, and she wasn't willing to give that up, not for anything or anyone.

Even Aaron.

She shot one last look at him in the rearview mirror, sprinting out of the building with a bucketful of water. She couldn't risk letting him break her heart again, not after how long she had been hung up on him before. Whether she liked it or not, it was all on her now—all on her to take down the men who had driven her from Kings Mountain for a second time.

It was time for her to bring Ziegler and the others down and she knew she wouldn't be able to do that if she stayed here. Aaron, Xavier, and Lawson meant well but ultimately, she needed to be involved and if they wouldn't let her do that, she needed to leave. With a final deep breath to steady her erratic heartbeat, she set her hands on the steering wheel and her eyes on the road ahead of her.

She put her foot down, set her eyes on the road in front of her, and took off away from the sanctuary as fast as she could. She felt the sobs rack her body, but she kept driving. All she could think about was him—the man she was being pulled away from all over again, the man she wasn't sure she would ever be able to forget.

Chapter Eighteen

Aaron could hardly believe what he was seeing as he stood there in front of the paddock. The whole thing was ablaze, and it was obvious someone had done this on purpose. But who? And why?

And where the hell had Bailey gone?

"Aaron, come on!" Cade yelled, gesturing for him to use the water in his bucket to put out some of the fire. Aaron blinked, reminding himself where he was, and then tossed the water over some of the flames in front of him. They had to work with what they had right now, and that wasn't much. Hannah was bringing over a hose, but that would only reach so far. In the main building itself, they might have been able to handle a fire of this magnitude, but out here, it was hard to imagine how they were going to deal with it.

He sprinted back toward the main building, the smell of smoke thick in the air. Everyone was up and working hard, most of them still in their pajamas, some even barefoot. This wasn't the kind of event where you could just take your time to get dressed before you dealt with it. No, it was a now-or-never kind of thing, and if they missed their chance, it would be a disaster.

It had been sunny for a few days, so the leaves of the

trees in the forest nearby were basically perfect kindling. It would just take one swift breeze, and the whole thing could go up in smoke. And then the cabins, then the lodge...damn, this was bad. This was really, really bad.

He filled up another bucket as River raced past him, Hannah in tow. He could already tell that they were going to get the horses. They loved those beautiful creatures, and they would likely be freaked out by the fire, even if they weren't in the direct line of it right now.

Aaron filled the bucket up as quickly as he could, and rushed back to the paddock. A line of men was forming to pass buckets back and forth as fast as possible, but the fire was spreading faster than they could contain it. Lawson was in the midst of it, directing the buckets, and he had to cover his mouth to keep from inhaling too much smoke. He was going to need to be careful.

"Lawson, I'll swap out with you in five minutes!" Aaron yelled to him over the noise of the crackling fire behind him. Lawson shook his head.

"I'm fine!" he yelled back.

Aaron rushed to him and grabbed his arm. "The smoke!" he reminded him. "You have to take a break! Five minutes, okay?"

"Fine, go!" Lawson replied, gesturing for him to head back to the building. He did as he was told, filling another bucket and bringing it back to the scene of the crime.

Xavier just stood there, looking shaken. His eyes were wide as he tried to take it all in. Aaron felt for him—this place was his home, the home he had made for himself and other people who had struggled like he had, and it was literally going up in smoke right before his eyes.

"Xavier!" Aaron called to him, grabbing his shoulder. "You can't just stand there. You need to do something!"

Xavier blinked, and then seemed to come back into himself. It was important he was in the midst of it. He commanded the most respect at Warrior Peak, and if people saw him panicking, they would panic.

"You go to Hannah and River, help them with the horses," he told Aaron.

Aaron nodded and took off toward the barn where the horses had been staying that night. Thank God they hadn't been in there when the fire had broken out. He wasn't sure the women would have been able to handle it. Bailey would have been devastated.

Thinking of Bailey, he glanced around, trying to see her. She had to be back at the main building, right? Helping out with the water? Had she been the one to raise the alarm when this fire had started? And if she was, why had she been out of bed in the middle of the night?

But before he could linger too long on that thought, he heard a horse let out a startled whinny, and he forced himself to focus on the matter at hand. The women needed his help, and he wasn't going to leave them to deal with this alone.

"Hey, Wheatie, chill!" Hannah called to the horse, who had reared up on her hind legs as soon as she had caught sight of the fire. Aaron quickly caught River's arm and pulled her away before Wheatie brought her hooves down a little too close for comfort.

"It's okay, she's just freaked because of the fire," Aaron told them. "There are some reins in the barn, let's get them on the horses and lead them as far away from this as we can, all right?"

"All right," Hannah replied, and they rushed toward the barn to grab the reins.

Aaron could smell oil in the air, the thick scent telling him this had been a deliberate, calculated attack. The people who had done this hadn't just wanted to cause a scene or scare them, they had wanted to cause real, long-term destruction. They had waited for the perfect night to do it—dry with a slight breeze.

A few licks of flame had already caught on to some of the low-hanging branches near the paddock. The flowers that Bailey, Hannah, and River had planted had already been swallowed by the flames entirely, nothing but ashes now.

Aaron looped the reins around Wheatie's head, and she let out a snort in protest. He planted a hand on her neck, trying to soothe her.

"Hey, girl, it's going to be all right," he tried to assure her. He hoped his tone of voice would be enough to soothe her, even though she must have known something was wrong. Horses were incisive at the best of times, and it wouldn't take much for them to start to really freak out. If they did, it would be chaos—panicked horses galloping around on top of everything else would only add to how hard this was going to be for them.

He led Wheatie slowly but surely away from the fire, grabbing the reins of another horse as he went. Hannah and River were close behind him, each with another horse, Hannah talking to River as though doing her best to keep her calm and focused.

He could smell the acrid smoke in the air as they reached the far end of the other paddock. Tying up the reins of the horses, Aaron hardly waited before he bolted back toward the fire once more.

"Lawson, out!" he roared toward Lawson, as he saw him still standing by the edge of the paddock. His face was covered in ash—only his eyes peered out from the smudges across his skin. He seemed to know better than to argue with Aaron, so he quickly nodded and turned his back, allowing Aaron to take his spot.

Aaron wrapped his fingers around his sleeve and pulled hard, tearing away the seam so he could wrap it around his face. It wouldn't do much, but it might be enough to keep him from getting too badly injured by the smoke inhalation. He had attended a few arsons cases in his time, and he knew that the smoke was what really got people. He'd seen what it could do, and he wasn't about to let that happen to him.

Xavier was still at the far end of the paddock, directing people. A line was passing buckets back and forth quickly, and Hannah rushed toward Xavier, checking that he was okay.

There was only so much they could do on their own. Getting one side of the field under control was a start, but the fire had started to spread rapidly through the trees. A few burning leaves had dropped to the ground, and the dry grass was beginning to catch fire.

"We need buckets over here!" Aaron yelled to the crew, waving one of them over so he could try and handle at least some of the inferno. His own cabin was only a few hundred feet away, and it wouldn't take long for the fire to reach it if he didn't get it under control.

He grabbed a full bucket and dashed into the forest, splashing the water wherever he saw the flames. He couldn't do much about the trees above him, but if he could stop the fire spreading through the forest floor, it might do the job.

But soon, he ran out of water, and he had to return to grab another one. The paddock was completely consumed now, either in flames or in the ashen remains of what had once been the fence and the building he'd spent so long putting together. He hated seeing the work he'd done reduced to nothing, but he would have time to think about that later. Right now, all that really mattered was making sure he stopped this before anyone got hurt.

"I'll help you," River told him, grabbing a bucket and following Aaron back to the forest. But just as she reached it, someone called her name.

"River, watch out!"

Aaron spun around just in time to see a heavy, flaming branch crash down from a tree, nearly landing on River's head. She dived out of the way just in time, managing to aim the water in her bucket at the branch to put it out. Cade rushed over to her, then dropped to his knees to pull her into his arms.

"Are you okay?" he demanded.

She nodded shakily. "Go," she told him. "I'm fine. We have more important things to worry about right now."

Cade dropped a kiss on her head, and River followed him back to the main building to grab another bucket of water as Aaron went about putting out the small patches of flames catching on the scorched earth. It would take the forest so long to recover from this, so long to regenerate back to its former glory. If they didn't stop this fire, it would damage far more than just the forest. Hopefully they would hear sirens soon and could leave the firefighting to the professionals.

He finished dumping the bucket and ran out of the woods again, past an exhausted-looking Xavier. He was breathing hard, sweat sheening his brow as he looked out over the seemingly hopeless fire in front of them.

He caught Aaron's eye, and his face darkened. He gestured at the paddock, now consumed with the inferno that he wasn't sure they would be able to control.

"This wasn't an accident, Aaron!" he yelled to him.

Aaron nodded in unspoken agreement. There was no way to deny it. This hadn't been an accident. Someone had come here to make sure they knew they weren't safe.

But until they got the fire under control, they couldn't even worry about that yet.

Aaron covered his mouth from the choking smoke and ran back to the lodge, his legs burning and his lungs scorching with each and every breath.

And, in the midst of it all, all he could think about was how much he hoped Bailey was safe.

Chapter Nineteen

Bailey stared at the skyline in her rearview mirror. It had started to glow orange now from the intensity of the fire burning up the property she had just run away from. Even winding her way down the mountain and toward the town, she could see it. The whole damn county probably could.

She slammed her foot on to the brakes, cursing herself. She hissed through her teeth. How could she turn her back on them? On Aaron? What kind of person was she? She couldn't just leave like this. They needed all the help they could get right now, and she would be damned if she walked away from her friends when they needed her. No matter what happened, she couldn't leave them to deal with the fire alone.

She looked over her shoulder, and was about to throw the truck into Reverse when a van came out of nowhere and smashed into the side of her truck. She hardly had time to process being hit before the truck spun off the road, dipping into the ditch at the far side and then tipping over on to its hood.

She pressed her hands to the sides of the cabin to try and brace for impact, gritting her teeth and tensing her body. A vehicle like this was probably too old for airbags, so she didn't have to worry about being blasted by one of them. Yet, that could end up being a bad thing, too. If the airbag had been there and deployed, it would have softened some of the abuse her body was taking now.

The truck bounced down the steep incline at the side of the road, crashing through a thicket of trees and bushes. Branches stabbed through the shattered windows, and one caught Bailey on the shoulder, digging into her flesh and leaving a deep gash through her shirt and into her skin. She cried out in pain, but the noise was lost over the sound of crumpling metal and the trees around her.

Finally, the truck came to a halt. Bailey breathed hard, the adrenaline coursing through her system. She could barely feel her fingers or toes, and she knew shock must be taking hold. But she needed to get out of the vehicle as quickly as possible. She didn't know what had been damaged in the accident, and she wasn't going to wait around to see. She needed to get out.

The accident. It felt wrong for her to even think of it that way, because she sure as hell knew it wasn't an accident. There wasn't much activity on this mountain road this time of night. There was nothing out this way except Warrior Peak Sanctuary. It wasn't like another vehicle wouldn't have seen her driving down the road, either. No, they must have been lying in wait for whoever tried to leave. Apparently, they didn't intend to let anyone escape tonight, blocking off their only route away from the lodge as soon as they had set the fire.

Once Bailey had managed to calm herself some, she checked around to see the best way out. The truck had landed on its side, so she would have to scramble out of the driver's side and climb up and out of the smashed window on the passenger one. She unclipped her seat belt, the wound in her shoulder throbbing, blood coursing down her arm to her hand. It was so slippery that it took her a moment to press the release button on her seat belt, but it finally sprang free.

Using her good arm, she pushed herself upright, then removed her jacket. There were a lot of glass shards still hanging from the broken window, so she'd need to use it to wipe away what was left in order to get out. She tied her jacket around her waist and then, using the steering wheel, dashboard, and driver's seat as a ladder, pushed and pulled her way through the truck to the window.

She suddenly thought she smelled gasoline, and paused to look around. She didn't see any flames, but if there was a leak in here, she really didn't have any time to waste at all. Clenching her jaw, she renewed her climb to the opposite window and wrapped her jacket around her fist to clear away the glass still clinging to the edges. She was already injured, but she didn't need to make it worse by getting broken pieces of glass embedded in her.

Bailey hoisted herself up to where she was hanging half in and half out of the truck over the window sill, and shimmied and pushed her way through. She braced for the hard landing as the ground suddenly came up to meet her. She lay on the cold ground for a moment, catching her breath, and realized there was nothing but dead silence surrounding her. She slowly sat up and looked around to check if the people who had done this to her were lying in wait. If they were, she couldn't see them anywhere close.

Taking a deep breath, she pulled herself up to standing, then started making her way back to the road, straining her ears for any noise of someone approaching. It was a slow process with her leg not completely healed, now aching more, and the throbbing in her shoulder and blood loss. She had to put pressure on the wound, but she needed both hands to help her balance and climb.

She also needed to get back to Warrior Peak, to make sure Aaron and the others were okay. She couldn't believe she had left them. She would never have ended up in that truck on the side of the road with a gash five inches long in her shoulder if she had just stuck around to help them fight the fire.

Reaching the road, she collapsed to her knees and leaned forward to rest her hands on the pavement as she caught her breath. With her new injury, how long would it take her to get up the mountain? She could already feel herself getting a little dizzy as she sat there. What if she couldn't make it back to the lodge? What if nobody noticed she was gone—or worse, what if they noticed she was gone but didn't come looking for her? Hell, someone might have seen her driving away from the fire and think she had started it. She hoped they wouldn't think that badly of her.

She tried to stand up, but it seemed like her body didn't want to cooperate. It took a couple of tries before she could successfully manage to get back on her feet. Her knees were trembling, and her hand was sticky with blood, but she grabbed her jacket and tied it around the wound as best she could, hoping it would do enough to stem the bleeding until she could get some real medical attention.

Looking back toward the dim glow of the fire on the

horizon, she steeled herself for what was to come. She had to get back to Aaron. It might not be easy, but she had to do it. She had to make sure he was okay.

And she had to tell him how sorry she was for even thinking about leaving him and Warrior Peak.

But before she could start her journey, a sudden light blinded her. She lifted her hands to shield her eyes, but she could still barely see. Two headlights blazed from the other side of the road—the van that had hit her. Her heart dropped and her lungs seized.

She tried to take a step but her legs gave way and she crashed to her knees again, still hiding her eyes from the glare of the bright light in front of her. Her entire body was pumping with adrenaline and she felt sick. She tried to tell herself it wasn't going to be as bad as she thought. Maybe these guys were just here to help. That could be true, right? Maybe they had been rushing up to Warrior Peak to help with the fire, and this had really just been nothing other than a terrible accident.

Lifting her head once more, she managed to make out two figures coming toward her. Their silhouettes cut through the near-white light from the headlights of the van. Didn't they know she could hardly see? She tried to call out to them, but her tongue was thick and heavy, and she was so nauseous she was going to be sick. She gagged and coughed but no words came out.

They had to be here to help her.

She lifted a hand, pointing in the direction of the lodge. She needed them to understand.

"Warrior Peak Sanctuary," she rasped, her voice tiny as she tried to force sound out of her lips. "You need to call someone, get help. There's a fire…"

"Oh, we know."

The sound of that voice froze the blood in her veins. Her body responded before her mind did and she heaved herself to the side and vomited in front of his shoes.

"Damn it!" He growled at her and shoved her back.

Bailey's ears started ringing and black dots danced before her eyes. She knew who that was. She tried to lift her head to look at him, but her eyesight was blurry and she felt too weak. She could just see his dark figure towering over her, outlined against the headlights behind him.

The sliding door of the van opening reached her ears, then two more sets of footsteps approached. The others were coming, all four of them were here to finish her off. She tried to turn to crawl back down the ledge, but her entire body had seized up. She wasn't sure if it was the pain or the fear or a mixture of both, but she couldn't move. All she could do was sit there as she waited for this nightmare to come to an end.

All four men advanced on her now, just like they had the night they had attacked her in the bar parking lot. Back then, at least, she had been able to run—she had had somewhere she could run to. But now? Now, she wasn't so sure. With Aaron and the others at the sanctuary fighting the fire these men had started, no one even knew she was gone. She didn't even know if any of them would survive the inferno. Her truck was wrecked, she was injured, and felt like she was on the verge of passing out. She had no means of escape and nowhere to go if she managed to get away. Which in her condition, was unlikely. She was at the mercy of the criminals before her and she was all alone.

The man who had spoken dropped down to his

haunches in front of her, inspecting her like a predator would inspect their prey. She recoiled from him, her hands sinking into the dirt at the side of the road, but she couldn't get far enough away. She could finally make out his face now, the hard smile that twisted his lips as he watched her with amusement. She tried again to push herself away again, but her body was done. Between the wreck, her injury, the blood loss, and the adrenaline crash, she had nothing left.

He grabbed her arm, the one with the gash, and she let out a loud groan of pain. She felt the throb of that agony racing through her whole system at once, her eyes rolling back as the shock of it took control of her.

"Good to see you again, Masters," Ziegler snarled, as he yanked her to her feet. She groaned again, stumbling as her body screamed in protest. She wanted to rip her arm from his grasp, but she didn't have the strength. All she could do was hang there like a rag doll and pray he finished her off quickly. Her body was utterly wrung out from everything she had endured. She couldn't even find the words to tell him what she thought of him and his cronies and what they'd done.

He leaned in close, a grin on his face that didn't reach his eyes.

"Thanks for making this so easy for us," he said, sneering.

With that, he shoved her toward the other men as everything faded to black, the headlights still burning the back of her vision.

Chapter Twenty

"Take the last of the buckets around to the other corner!" Xavier called to the group, and a few men hurried to take a couple more buckets full of water to the far edge of the paddock. Aaron breathed a sigh of relief as soon as he saw them douse out the last of the flames. It was over, thank God.

Everyone was shaken, but nobody was actually hurt, which had to count for something. The horses were okay, too, though it would take a while for them to fully settle again. The fire hadn't reached the main lodge, and the county fire services had finally arrived and managed to put it out at the edge of the forest. Everything was under control for the time being.

Aaron sank down to the grass for a moment to catch his breath, and unwrapped the sleeve he had tied around his mouth. Tilting his head back, he drew in a deep lungful of air. Not exactly clear yet, but the smoke was at least starting to fade now.

Everyone had backed off to a safe distance now that the fire was actually contained, and he scanned the group, searching for Bailey. He hadn't seen her since that brief moment when the fire first started, but she must have been out there helping, right? It was all such a blur.

But, as he looked around, his heart started to hammer in his chest again. Where was she? He couldn't see her anywhere. He hurried toward the crowd that had formed near the front entrance to the main lodge, hoping she was just buried somewhere toward the back—she couldn't be missing. Not on the night of this fire. It would have been too much of a coincidence, and he knew she wouldn't have walked away from them right now unless she had a really good reason.

Or, unless someone forced her to.

"River, Hannah," he called to the women when he spotted them together.

They both turned to greet him.

"Hey, what's up?" Hannah called back. Her face looked drawn and worried, and he wondered if she had noticed that Bailey was missing, too.

"Have you seen Bailey?" he asked them.

They exchanged a look, and then shook their heads.

"Haven't seen her," River replied. "Why? Is something wrong?"

He shook his head, panic starting to rise. He needed to find her, right the hell now. He could feel it in his chest, how bad it would be if he didn't locate her. He couldn't let anything happen to her. Not after he had given up so much to keep her safe in the first place.

"You're looking for Bailey, right?" one of the guys asked. He was a relatively new arrival at the lodge, and Aaron didn't know much about him, but if he had some information about Bailey, he was going to hear it.

"Yeah, yeah, I am," he replied. "Have you seen her?"

"I saw her driving off a few minutes after the fire

started," he replied, pointing down toward the road that led away from Warrior Peak. "In that direction."

Damn. Aaron's mind was racing. Why would she leave? Had she done it willingly, or had she been forced? The last conversation they'd had was an argument, and he hated the thought of her fleeing so soon after their disagreement. He thought it was something they could work through, but maybe she felt differently.

"I noticed her truck still here. You sure she took off?" Xavier asked, cutting into the conversation. His brow was furrowed, and he looked concerned.

"Seems like it. I saw her a moment at the start of the fire, but haven't been able to find her since," Aaron replied. "She must have snagged a lodge truck so we wouldn't know she was gone." His eyes darkened. Looks like she was running away this time. That thought made his chest ache.

"Then you need to find out where she's headed," he replied. "It's not safe for her to be on her own right now. This fire starting out of nowhere can't be a coincidence, either. And so soon after you fill us in on your past and finding out dirty cops know of your location. We can only assume they know Bailey was here, too. It's got to have something to do with why she left. Maybe they contacted her in some way?"

Aaron nodded in agreement. That made sense. If Ziegler or one of the others had found a way to contact Bailey and made threats against Warrior Peak or even him, she would have left to protect everyone here.

Xavier tossed him a set of keys. "Here, take my car," he told him. "We'll be waiting. And call if you need backup."

"Thanks. I will," Aaron replied.

With that, he made his way toward the car, his mind running so fast he didn't know how to control it. As he climbed in and drove off, his thoughts were frantic, his entire system consumed with the fear of what might have happened to her.

He stared at the road ahead of him as he drove, willing himself not to screw this up—not to make more of a mess of this than he already had. He should have checked on her after what had happened the night before. He knew she was upset about the guys at the sanctuary wanting her to stand down and let them handle it. She thought they all saw her as lesser than, incapable. But she wasn't thinking clearly, letting her emotions override reason. They knew she could handle herself—that wasn't it at all.

With their backgrounds, though, they were protectors at their core and if they could stand between someone else and danger—they'd do it every time. The guys were also thinking of her future. If Bailey wanted to stay in law enforcement, she needed to be removed from all of this. Not have this black mark on her record where anyone could question her motives.

The road wound down the mountain, and he drove as quickly as he could without throwing the car off the side when he took the corners. He just needed to get to her. She couldn't have gotten far, right? She didn't know the area well—unless she had done her planning before she left, and made sure she knew where she was going. And she had never been the kind of woman who would walk directly into something without knowing what she was facing.

He gripped the wheel tight, his whole body rigid with

tension. He would find her. He *would* find her. And if Ziegler and his crew had put themselves in the middle of this, he would take them all out on the spot and bring them down for good, as long as it meant she was safe. He would not fail her this time.

He had blown up his life to make sure she was okay—and blown up hers in the process. Both of them had given up so much, lost so much time with each other and the thought of losing more just because these villains couldn't just leave them alone... He didn't know what to make of it all. He and Bailey were both out of the picture, no one else knew what they did, so why could Ziegler and the rest just not move on? Were they that far gone with their power and corruption that they thought they had to eliminate them permanently? He just couldn't wrap his mind around that.

Whatever their reasoning, though, there wasn't a chance in hell he was going to let anything happen to her.

And if she had left of her own volition? What then? If she was okay, he felt like he should be fine with it, but the two of them had something he didn't want to give up quite so soon. He wasn't entirely sure what their connection was, or if she would even want to pursue it after everything that had happened, but he knew he would do anything to make it work. He had waited so long before, and now she was finally back. How could he pass up that chance?

He rounded a bend in the road, and slammed on the brakes, taking in the scene before him. Down the embankment on the left side, near the tree line, was the lodge truck—it looks like it had flipped off the road, rolling and sliding nearly twenty feet before coming to a smoking stop on its side. His gut clenched at the sight. He quickly scanned the area but didn't see any movement near the crashed vehicle. He hoped Bailey made it out in one piece, or there'd be hell to pay. On the right side of the road, sitting at an angle facing the embankment with the headlights still blazing, was a van with a dented front bumper.

He turned off the car's headlights and quietly pulled behind the van, making sure his car was hidden behind the glow of the headlights. He didn't know what was going on here, but he wanted to make sure he had as much time as he could to work it out before anyone else spotted him. He got the feeling he was going to have to take every advantage he could.

He silently got out and looked around. It was pitch black out here, the only light coming from the headlights. If he stayed low and moved quickly, he'd be able to cross the road without being seen. Keeping his steps as soft as possible while hurrying, he made his way to the opposite side of the road and down to the crashed truck, praying she would still be inside. Even if she was hurt, he could get her back to the sanctuary and patch her up. But if she was gone, what the hell could he do about it? Would he even be able to get her back? He immediately shut that thought down.

If Ziegler and his crew were the ones to have caused this and had taken her to parts unknown, Aaron knew he'd move heaven and earth to find her and get her back to the safety of Warrior Peak with him, where she belonged. He wasn't giving up, no matter what he had to do or where he had to go. No matter how long it took, he'd find her.

The truck was empty when he peered inside through the windshield, but he did see blood. He took a moment and looked around to see if there were any signs to indicate she had managed to get away, but there were no visible clues as to where she went in the immediate area.

Looking back at the truck, he noticed a lot of blood smeared across the seatbelt and door handle. Seeing both, he knew Bailey was at least badly injured and he needed to get to her soon. The passenger side window, which was facing upright, was smashed, so she could have crawled out or someone could have pulled her out. Either way, she wasn't there, so she had to have at least survived the crash. He had to believe that. So where was she now?

He tried to think what he would do if this had been him, but his mind kept going back to all the blood inside the truck. Yes, the truck had tumbled down the embankment so he'd expect some, but not as much as he'd seen inside. If that was any indication of how she was doing, Bailey needed him now.

Or else...

No, he couldn't even let himself think that. He wouldn't let his mind go there. He had to trust she had been able to find a way out of this, no matter how bad it might look. He knew he didn't give her enough credit for what a badass she was—none of them did. She could handle so much more than her small stature indicated.

Giving up on his search at the truck, Aaron quietly made his way back toward the road, keeping his steps light and his head down. That van had run her off the road, he was sure of it. There was no way she would have crashed without cause. She was a careful driver, even when she was under stress. And if someone had wanted to take her out like this, who was to say what else they would do to make sure she played by their rules?

He sank down by the edge of the road, looking back and forth, trying to figure out who was here and what they might have been doing. He didn't want to make his presence known until he had a better idea of what was going on. Nobody would be coming up to Warrior Peak unless they had a good reason to. Someone might have tried to play hero with the fire, but he doubted it. It was impossible to see anything down this far, apart from the smoke in the sky.

Around him, he couldn't make out anything but the usual sounds of the night. The van was still running, so whoever was out there was planning on using it for a fast retreat once they finished whatever they were doing. Since he couldn't find her below at the wreck, he had to assume the *whatever* had something to do with Bailey and why he hadn't seen her around. He wasn't going to walk away from this until he knew for sure what was going on.

He was about to move to a different angle when he heard it. The sound of a struggle—of voices. Mostly men, but he could also hear a woman saying something, protesting. Much to his relief, it sounded like Bailey.

He kept a watchful eye pinned to the van opposite him. He felt his heart pounding in his chest, and he took long, deep breaths, trying to settle himself before he freaked out too badly. He couldn't rush this. He had made decisions based on his emotions before, and that rarely ended well for him.

Suddenly, he saw a commotion near the van. Just for a split second, four familiar figures shoved Bailey toward the back. They were trying to kidnap her! God only knew what they would do if they managed to get her out of there, but he wasn't going to let that happen. He had to stop it.

He rose to his feet and took a deep breath. *Now or never.* If they got her into that van, it was over, and he wasn't going to let the woman he loved be lost to him a second time.

Without another thought, he went sprinting toward them, blazing with all the anger of a bat out of hell and ready to put these guys down. For good.

Chapter Twenty-One

"Let go of me!" Bailey yelled as she tried to yank herself away from Benning. He had her arm in a viselike grip, twisted up her back, and the pain was throbbing so badly from the gash in her shoulder she thought she might pass out. One of the men had ripped the tourniquet she had made with her jacket off her arm, probably wanting to cause her more pain. She felt the blood leaking down her arm again and dripping off her fingers onto the ground. If she didn't think of something soon, she wouldn't be able to put up much of a fight at all. She'd already lost a lot of blood and was feeling dangerously woozy. She didn't know how much longer she even had.

"You already tried that, remember? You're only hurting yourself more," Ziegler remarked to her, his voice laced with a mocking amusement. She tried to turn to him, her eyes dark with anger, but Benning had too strong a grip on her. She couldn't fight them off.

"Really, Bailey, you should leave the hurting to us," Moore added with a laugh, the others joining in.

Sheer terror took hold of her as she realized their intent. *I can't fight them off.*

Ziegler and Benning were pushing and dragging her toward the van, where Moore and Lee stood by the sliding door, waiting to help force her inside. What were they going to do with her when they managed to get her out of here? Her mind spun with all the hideous possibilities, and she couldn't stand the thought of letting them get to her like that.

She was shoved toward the van again, but the physical manhandling didn't seem to be enough for these guys. No, they wanted to really hurt her—they wanted to make sure she suffered. She hadn't even exposed them, she just hadn't gone along with their twisted plans. She didn't even want to think what might happen if they found out she had actually been scheming against them.

"You really thought you could stop us?" Ziegler said, sneering at her as he grabbed a handful of her hair and yanked her head around in his direction. "After you've been away so long? After your precious boyfriend sent you packing for desk work for years on end?"

She felt the tears blurring her eyes, and she tried to blink them back, not wanting them to see how much they were getting to her. *Aaron.* If they got her out of here, she would never see Aaron again, she was sure of it. Even though she had almost made the same decision herself tonight, she could clearly see now how much of a mistake it was. She couldn't let that happen.

"You're nothing," Ziegler continued, jerking on her hair, clearly enjoying her distress. "And your boyfriend is going to go down for this, too. We might have left him alone if you hadn't run crying to him."

The tears racked her body now. She had brought this to his door again, she had made it so he couldn't be safe. If she had just kept her distance, not been so stubborn thinking she could fix everything, it never would have gone down the way it had. She couldn't believe she had been so foolish. She—a rookie cop who ended up riding a desk for six years—thought she could end this, when Aaron—a sergeant on the police force, a seasoned officer, and the best man she had ever known—hadn't even been able to succeed. What did she think she would be able to do against these men?

As the fear and dread set in, all of this started to feel as though it was happening to someone else. Like she was watching herself as it happened, not in her own body. And, when she saw it like that, the anger was what rose to the top. All of this was so unfair. All she had ever wanted was to be a good cop, and they had taken that from her. They had taken her chance to live out the career she had wanted, the life she had wanted—with the man she wanted, too.

Before she could think it through, she spat at Ziegler. "You're never going to get away with this."

He smirked at her. "I already have," he replied smugly.

"I know you've managed all this time, but that was before you let me know about it," she continued. "You know how many people there are working on this case? Not just cops, either—former military and former CIA agents. There's so much crap coming your way, you don't have any idea."

They fell silent for a moment, and Benning and Ziegler exchanged a look. Both of them actually looked…worried. Like there was something to be really afraid of. A swell of pride filled her chest as she watched them. Yeah, they should be scared. They should be downright terrified at the storm that was coming their way. They might have thought taking her out would stop it, but it was only just getting started.

And she couldn't wait to see it rip them apart. If she was still around, that is.

But before she could continue rubbing it in, Benning pulled a gun from his holster. He pressed it against her side, and she tried to pull away from him, so then he leveled it straight at her head. She immediately froze, and time stood still. She wanted to shift away but all she could see was the black barrel looking back at her. Unflinching, unwavering.

She had never been on the other end of a gun like this. They had flashed a knife at her before, of course, but that had been different. This? This was the end. One wrong move and she would be dead. Of course, some part of her had known they were going to do this eventually.

Her life flashed before her eyes as Benning wrapped his other hand around the gun. The other men were dead silent, like even they hadn't been prepared for this to happen. The tears were gone now—she was too scared to cry. Her whole body was frozen in terror as she faced the reality of what was going to happen to her.

What had she even done with her life? All she'd ever wanted to do was be a police officer. After sitting behind a desk for six years, she had finally gotten back to where she felt like she could make a difference, and these men had taken that away from her. She had spent those years so angry at Aaron for betraying her, but she understood that he was only trying to protect her from this. This moment right here. And now that they had found each other again, she realized that he was the only man she'd ever loved.

That was what she had done with her life: She had loved him so much more than she had ever loved anyone else. Even when it had been hard, even when they had been apart all of those years, she had never stopped loving him. Being with him was what she had dreamed of since she first met him, and she was glad that she had let him know that she loved him. That was something, at least.

"You don't speak to us like that," Benning spat at her. She heard his voice shaking. Was he really willing to do this? Kill another cop? Maybe she wasn't even the first. There must have been other people through the years, other people who had dared to get close to discovering their secrets. Maybe they had just killed all of them off, like they were about to do to her.

The thought of it was enough to make her sick. She would never get to see Aaron again, she would never get to apologize to him. Maybe they had been right, maybe it would have been better if she had stayed off the case, because look at what was happening to her. She had basically led them right to him, and she wasn't sure if they would stop after they had killed her.

"I'm sorry," she whispered under her breath. She knew he couldn't hear her, but it didn't matter. She had to believe there was a way for him to know how she really felt. She had to believe she could take her leave from this life without fearing that he didn't understand how much she cared for him. She always had, even when she had also hated him.

"You bitch," Benning snarled.

Bailey inhaled a deep breath, bracing herself for what was about to come.

And then, the gun went off. She jumped, and waited for the blackness to hit her. She fell back into the van and squeezed herself into a ball so they couldn't take another shot. The pain would come any second now. Where had the bullet hit? She could still feel the throbbing in her shoulder, but...

She lifted her head and looked at her body. No fresh wounds, other than the ones she'd gotten from the crash. And no bullet holes, either. She slowly sat upright. Outside, through the ringing in her ears, she heard chaos. Shouting, banging, crashing, the low, heavy sound of punches being landed. What was going on? Had they turned on each other, or...?

She slid to the edge of the van, and her eyes widened when she figured out what was actually happening. They were fighting—but not with each other, with Aaron. Aaron seemed to have already taken Ziegler and the others down, but Benning was still on his feet, holding the gun.

"Back off, Ward!" he barked at him. "If you know what's good for you—"

But before he could get out another word, Aaron lunged at him, dropping his head and slamming it into Benning's chest. The force of the impact knocked the gun out of his hands, sending it flying across the ground and into the tall grass. Bailey couldn't make out what happened after that, but judging by the sounds of their struggle, it wasn't going Benning's way.

When she got the nerve to peer around the van, she saw Aaron getting to his feet, wiping away sweat from his brow before he turned his attention back to her.

She felt herself collapse the moment before he reached

her. All the emotion, all the fear, facing down death—it all fell away the minute he wrapped his arms around her, holding her tight, as though he never wanted to let her go.

"You're okay," he murmured to her, his voice soft in her ear. She knew they couldn't stay long. It was only a matter of time before the guys came to, and they needed to be as far from here as possible. But right now, all she wanted to do was press herself into his arms.

"Oh my God," she gasped, hardly able to think straight. The sound of the gunshot was still ringing in the air around them, and it was at that moment she remembered the gun.

"Aaron, the gun," she squeaked to him. "You need to get the gun—"

"This gun, you mean?"

Aaron spun around, protecting her with his whole body without thinking. She cowered behind him. She wanted to help, but she feared Benning might take the shot he had missed the first time.

"This little reunion is nice, isn't it?" he said, sneering at the two of them. Bailey heard such cruelty in his voice, she had no idea how she had been able to miss it before. All of it seemed so obvious to her now, the reality of what they had done, how far they had gone. That they would kill her and Aaron if they got the chance.

"Stay away from her," Aaron snarled, and Benning cocked the gun. The sound of the click echoed through the air around them, a threat.

"You going to make me?" Benning asked.

Before Bailey had a chance to hold him back, Aaron dived at Benning again, shoving him to the ground and picking up right where he had left off with the fight.

Chapter Twenty-Two

Aaron reached for the gun, managing to knock it out of Benning's hand for a moment. Lee was stirring next to him, coming back from the hit Aaron had dealt him to the back of the head with a rock he'd found on the road. He had to subdue them both, and keep them away from Bailey. He knew one thing for damn sure: He wasn't going to let them get away with this anymore.

"Damn," Benning snarled as he rolled out from underneath Aaron and scrambled back toward the weapon.

"Aaron!" Bailey yelled from the van, but Aaron held his hand up.

"You stay right there," he told her. "I can handle this."

He gritted his teeth, and repeated the same thing to himself. He *could* handle this. He just had to keep pushing forward, keep doing what he could to bring this nightmare to an end.

All he could think about was the way Bailey had been trembling in his arms. He didn't want her to feel that fear for another moment, and he would do anything to end it. She didn't deserve this, and the only way he could stop these men from hurting her again would be to take them out for good.

Lee was on his feet again, and Aaron rounded on him,

pushing him back against the van, next to Bailey. He crashed into it, still woozy from the blow he had taken to his head, and his entire body shuddered with the pain.

But he had a knife, and he reached for it quickly, pulling it out and flashing it at Aaron. Aaron sprang back, and Lee raised the knife, ready to swing down again.

Until Bailey swept his feet out from under him. Lee seemed to have forgotten she was there, and Aaron nodded to her in thanks. Just like old times, he knew he wouldn't have been able to do it without her by his side.

He turned his attention back to Benning again, his face tightening as he glared at him. Benning had managed to get the gun trained on him again, and Aaron ducked just in time to feel a bullet whizzing over his head. It hit the van with a loud clang, and Bailey let out a yelp of surprise. Aaron turned to make sure she hadn't been hit, but she was out of the van, her arms wrapped around Lee's neck as she held him in place and pushed the air out of him to subdue him once more.

She had him covered. Even though she was scared, and injured, she could still fight for herself. He lunged at Benning, who fired off another shot in a panic. There were only so many bullets in that magazine, and it wouldn't be long before he ran out entirely. And when he did, Aaron would make his move.

He dove into the tall grass for cover, making it so Benning couldn't see him to fire off another shot. His chest pressed to the ground, his whole body was rigid as he waited to make the next move. He didn't even know what he was going to do, but he had to do something.

He crawled along the ground as Benning paced around at the edge of the grass, trying to spot him. He probably would have just shot blindly if it hadn't been for the limited amount of ammo he had right now. He didn't have the support of the others, and he knew Aaron was well trained in how to handle himself and what he should do in these situations.

Only problem was, so was Benning. They'd likely been through the same training, and Benning was far more practiced when it came to a showdown like this one. Aaron shuffled through the grass, trying to make as little noise as possible, until he reached Benning.

He grabbed his feet and yanked hard, knocking the other man off-balance and sending him crashing to the ground. Benning let out a yell, but there was nothing he could do to fight it. His whole body fell like cement, landing with such a thump the air was knocked out of him.

Aaron used the moment he had before Benning got himself back together to dive for the gun and take it from him, then tossed it as far as he could into the tall grass behind them. He just wanted that thing away from him, away from Bailey. When he had seen Benning pointing it at her, that was the only thing he had been able to focus on.

Once it was gone, he scrambled away from Benning to get to Bailey again. She had Lee passed out at her feet, and she jumped up as soon as she saw him getting close. He threw his arms around her, pulling her in against him, pressing his face into her hair. He needed this. He needed her. He needed them together, no matter what he had to do to make it happen, no matter how hard it might be.

"You're okay, you're okay," he told her again. "I've got you. We can get you back up to the lodge, get you patched up—"

But before he could say another word, a sound rang out behind them. He stiffened—a gunshot. He could hear it burning in his ears. He should have kept the gun, but he had been in such a rush to get back to Bailey, he couldn't think about anything else.

And it might have just cost him everything.

"Aaron!" Bailey exclaimed as she pulled back. There was blood on her shirt, staining through, and for a second he thought somehow she had been shot. But then, as she reached out her hand to his torso, he realized that wasn't what had happened.

It was him who had taken the bullet.

"Aaron, get down," she pleaded, but he turned to shield her, refusing to let Benning take her down, too. The pain was starting to set in now, radiating through his body. He glanced down and saw the thick, wet rivulets of blood running down his jeans. He could hardly see straight, dark spots clouding his vision, but it didn't matter—he had to keep her safe. It was the only thing he could think of, regardless of what was happening to him. He wouldn't let anything happen to her.

If it was the last thing he did.

Finally, as the spots began to clear, he saw Benning walking toward them, limping slightly as though he was injured. But he had a grin on his face, as he advanced on the two of them.

And this time, Aaron didn't know if he had any more fight in him. If he could hold him off.

"Aaron," Bailey begged him, trying to pull him back down by her side, but he didn't move. He couldn't. It was as though his feet were rooted to the ground, every bone in his body telling him that the only thing that mattered was Bailey's safety. Just like he had done all those years ago, he would sacrifice himself to protect her.

"Get out of the way, Ward," Benning said, sneering at him. "You really want to leave her to die alone? Your shot was meant for her. Move so I can do her, too. That way, you can have your little romantic moment before you both go."

"Shut up," Aaron snarled back at him. "You're not getting past me." He never wanted to hear Benning talking about what he and Bailey had together. It was just for them.

He would never allow anything between the two of them to be sullied by what these monsters would say about them. Benning would never understand the love Aaron had for Bailey, anyway. Or the love she had for him in return. He was a man who scared women, a man who made them feel as though they weren't safe. He would never understand sacrificing everything for that person, doing anything to make sure they were protected and cared for.

"You sure?" Benning asked, cocking the gun again. How many bullets were left in there? Aaron eyed the barrel, contemplating his next move. But there was no way, no way he could win this. He was starting to feel woozy and tired from the blood loss. He wasn't going to make it much longer.

No matter all that had happened, though, Aaron had never imagined a cop would point a gun at him like this. Someone he was supposed to be brothers-in-arms with, no less.

But Benning clearly felt none of that for him. Benning had banded with a team like Ziegler and his cronies, men who would likely turn their backs on him the first chance they got.

That was something Aaron could take away from this, at least. Benning would never be happy. None of them would be. They had to live their lives looking over their shoulders, never able to rest, never able to slow down, never able to stop. Aaron had lived more than half a decade in peace, really finding comfort in himself and the choices he'd made—enough so that when Bailey came back into his life, he had been able to meet her and tell her how he really felt.

Benning pressed the gun against his chest. Then, a voice cut in from beside them.

"Wait. Let me."

Ziegler was on his feet again, standing there, holding out his hand for the gun. Even through it was clear Benning wanted to be the one to pull the trigger himself, he knew better than to argue with their leader, and he handed the gun over to him, pressing it into his palm.

Ziegler stepped forward and took his place in front of Aaron, grinning widely.

"I've been waiting for this for a long time," he spat. "See you, Ward."

Chapter Twenty-Three

Bailey didn't understand how they'd gotten here. They had gone from being in each other's arms, his voice in her ear promising her she was going to be okay, to this—to this man holding a gun against Aaron's head, ready to end him for good.

Bailey hid behind him, hanging on to him for dear life, arms wrapped around his waist and face pressed into his back. He would never let her take this bullet for him, that much she knew for sure, but she still didn't want to let him die without feeling her here with him. She loved him too much for that.

There had to be something she could do. As Ziegler took a breath and steadied up his shot, time slowed, spreading out before her and giving her a moment to gather herself. She had to make her move now, she knew that, but what could she do? She was right behind him. Could she make it out in time? She remembered what she had done to take down Lee, taking him out at the legs, and she knew she was going to have to pull the same thing again.

No time to think. Only time to act. And if she didn't move now, she and Aaron wouldn't be alive much longer.

She lunged out from behind Aaron, rolling down to

the left, and caught Ziegler's eye, drawing his attention from Aaron just long enough for her to drive a leg into his, sending him crashing to the ground. He squeezed the trigger, sending a bullet up above their heads, and Bailey rolled out of the way and under the van so it wouldn't hit her on the way down, crawling quickly to the other side.

A commotion had broken out around her again, and it took her a moment to realize that it wasn't Ziegler and the others causing it. No, this time, there were people here on their side. Xavier and Cade rushed past her, followed by Lawson, and a few men from the tactical team at the lodge. She scrambled to her feet, only interested in one thing: Aaron.

He had managed to make it to the back of the van, leaving the other highly trained people to take down the corrupt cops who had done this to them. Bailey checked on him, and found his face pale, his eyes distant.

"Here, put some pressure on this," she told him, linking her hands through his and pressing them into his wound.

And then, she heard Xavier yelling for help. When she turned, she saw Ziegler scrambling toward the gun where he had dropped it on the ground. She sprang up and dived toward it, kicking it out of his reach, and then grabbed it and let off the rest of the shots into the ground. She didn't want anyone else using this tonight.

She sank to her knees as the guys took down the cops, subduing them one by one until there was no fight left to be had. Xavier came over to her and offered her a hand, helping her up to her feet.

"How did you know?" she asked, and he shrugged.

"When Aaron went looking for you and didn't come

back, I figured something was up," he remarked. "And then when we heard the gunshots, we knew you must need our help."

"Thank you," she whispered softly to him. The words didn't feel strong enough for how grateful she really was. If it hadn't been for him, and the rest of the guys from Warrior Peak, she would have lost Aaron, and she knew she would never have been able to live with that.

She made her way back to the van, where Aaron had managed to prop himself up. He looked a little better now—his face wasn't quite as pale. Maybe the wound hadn't been as bad as she first thought.

"Bailey," he breathed, and he wrapped his spare arm around her and pulled her in close, pressing his face into her neck. She sank into him. It was over. It was really over. After everything that had happened, everything that they had been through, it was done. There was no way Ziegler and the rest of them were going to get away after this. They didn't stand a chance. Whatever they thought they had been capable of, they were wrong.

She could finally relax and just be with Aaron. She knew he was going to need some serious patching up—a bullet wound wasn't the kind of thing you messed around with—but he was alive. She could feel the slow rise and fall of his breath as Ziegler, Moore, Lee, and Benning were handcuffed and put into trucks, ready to be dropped off at the sheriff's office when they were done here.

"I thought something had happened to you in the fire," Aaron murmured to her, and she pulled her head back.

"Nothing happened to me then," she assured him, but she was certain he'd have more questions. Like why she'd left while everyone else was distracted with the fire. She wished she had a better answer for him than the truth, but she didn't see any way around it right now.

"I... I was just leaving," she admitted. "I thought I could go after them myself, I thought I could take them down. I didn't want to be pushed out of it again. I saw the fire, I let everyone know what was going on, and then I left."

He tensed.

"But I can see how wrong I was," she assured him. "They drove me off the road—that's why I crashed the truck. And if it hadn't been for you, they would have killed me."

She inhaled shakily as the reality of that hit her. Yes, they really would have killed her. If it hadn't been for him throwing himself into the fray the way he had, she would have been dead. The thought chilled her to the bone. She squeezed him tighter.

"And they told me...they told me they came looking for you because of me," she confessed. "And I'm so sorry for that, Aaron, I never meant for that to happen."

"Hey, you have nothing to apologize for," he told her, brushing her tears away. "I know how hard it's been for you. I know how much you wanted to take them down. And I know you probably could have done it yourself. I just wanted to help you. The only thing that matters to me is that you're all right."

She nodded, but she wasn't sure she totally believed him. Could he really be that quick to forgive her, after everything she'd done? She didn't know. She wanted to believe it, but she knew she had some explaining to do.

"I didn't want to go," she admitted to him. "I never did, Aaron. I just... I didn't want either of us getting hurt again, not after what happened before. And I thought if I made the decision for you, it wouldn't be something you had to...something you had to do for yourself, at least this time."

"That was one of the hardest things I've ever had to do," he murmured, shaking his head, eyes misty as though he was remembering it at that very moment.

She cupped his face in her hands. "I'm never going to be apart from you again," she told him fervently, surprising even herself with how sure she was of that fact. She scanned his face, eyes wide, needing him to understand how much she meant it.

"That sounds good to me," he agreed, and he drew her in for a kiss. Even with the slash in her shoulder, her body filled with pleasure at his touch. Here he was, the man she had wanted for all these years, the man she loved, and there was nothing in the way of them being together. It was finally just...them. Their pasts left far behind for once, a history they never even had to think about again. No matter what happened next, she could hold on to him, and she wanted that more than anything in the world.

She wrapped her arms around him and buried her face into his shoulder again, a wave of emotion crashing through her. He held her to his side, and she knew he was feeling everything she was right now. The two of them were together again, no matter what had pushed them apart, no matter what had landed them back in each other's lives. All the fight in her was gone, all the anger forgotten. Their pasts didn't matter now.

No, the only thing that mattered now was their future. And that they got to spend it together.

Chapter Twenty-Four

As Aaron held Bailey, he tried to let himself relax. She was safe. The guys were dealt with. Even though this bullet wound wasn't exactly making him feel fantastic right now, he knew it could be treated. He would have been dead by now if it was lethal.

"Hey, Aaron."

Lawson stood next to the van, waiting for them to break from their embrace. Aaron winced as he turned around to face him, doing his best to keep the pain from his face. He didn't want to worry anyone.

"We're going to get one of our guys to drive you down to town," he explained. "Xavier let Willis know what's going on, and they've got emergency personnel standing by at the hospital for you and Willis will meet you there. Cade and I will make sure this scum gets to the station to be locked up, once and for all. Bailey, you need medical attention, too." Lawson pointed at her. "You look about as bad as he does."

"Not quite." Xavier walked over and chimed in. "But you lost quite a bit of blood, too." He nodded at her shoulder. "That needs to be cleaned and treated as soon as possible."

"Thank you," Aaron replied, his voice coming out

weaker than it had before. He could see those dark spots at the side of his vision again, and he tried to blink them away.

"Aaron, are you all right?" Bailey asked, the worry evident in her voice as she pushed away some of his sweat-soaked hair from his face.

"I will be," he replied, and she offered him an arm to help him to his feet. He leaned on her heavily, and she draped one of his arms over her shoulder to help guide him to the car waiting to get them out of here.

It was carnage out on the road. Truck parts were scattered everywhere from the wreck, and Lee was making a scene, fighting hard to try and break free. He didn't stand a chance against the people around him, but he had never known when to give up.

Bailey managed to get Aaron into the car, and laid him out on the back seat. She climbed in behind him and put his head on her lap.

"It's going to be okay," she whispered to him, though there was some doubt in her voice. How bad was it? He planted his hand on the wound as the driver pulled away from the chaos around them, driving them the rest of the way down to the small town at the bottom of the mountain.

Aaron looked up at Bailey. For the first time since he had seen her on the side of the road, he noticed there was a mark on her arm—a wound, actually. Then he suddenly remembered the blood smeared in the overturned truck. She had been injured, and he was just recalling it. Getting to her, keeping her safe, taking down the guys... All of it was running together. But now that the adrenaline was leaving his system, he was remembering the rest.

He couldn't believe he'd forgotten that she'd been hurt, too. He lifted his head to look at it, and when she noticed him staring, she shook her head.

"It's nothing."

"Did they hurt you?"

"I just got a few scratches in the crash."

"A few scratches?" Aaron exclaimed. "That looks worse than a few damn scratches—"

"Please, Aaron, you need to rest," Bailey begged him, gently pressing on his shoulders to guide him back down to the spot he had been in before. He was going to make sure they were done and out for the count. He was going to do everything in his power to make sure they never got out of jail. Never had the chance to do something like this to anyone again.

His head pounded with anger, almost distracting him from the pain rushing through the rest of his system. He wanted to tear them apart, limb from limb. He wanted to make them pay for thinking they could dare lay a hand on the woman he loved.

"It's okay," she promised him. "I'm fine, really. I'll be healed up in a few weeks. It'll be like it never happened."

His jaw was still clenched, his body still tense at the thought of them doing that to her.

"Aaron, it's over," she reminded him gently, still running her fingers through his hair. "There's more than enough now to put them behind bars for good. They won't stand a chance after this. They're going to have to face the reality of what they've done, and you know how hard cops go after their own."

He nodded. She was right. When people found out what they had been doing, they would put them away for a long time. It would only be a start when it came to finding justice for the people who had been hurt by their crimes, of course, but it would be something. After so long fearing them, so long wondering if they were going to come after either him or Bailey, he never had to worry about that again.

"I know," he breathed back, and she leaned down to plant another kiss on his lips. He reached over to grip her hand tight, never wanting to let her go.

He settled his head back against her lap. He still felt the pain, but he could also feel himself starting to relax, feeling so tired...

"Aaron."

Bailey spoke his name again, and he could just about make her out through the fog enveloping him right now. He was exhausted all of a sudden. Maybe just the rush of adrenaline he'd needed to survive tonight, or maybe something else entirely, but his eyes were starting to droop.

"You need to stay awake," she told him, shaking him slightly. He managed to half open his eyes again, his gaze landing on her above him.

"I know," he mumbled.

"It's not going to take us long to get there," she promised him. "We just passed the restaurant we had dinner at, remember?"

He smiled at the memory. That was when he had kissed her for the first time. When they had told each other how they really felt, and slept together for the first time that night. No matter what happened next, he knew he would always be glad he got a chance to share that with her. He never wanted to forget how it felt for her to tell him to kiss her, just like he had imagined a million times over the years.

"I remember," he replied, but his words came out a little slurred. She tightened her grip on him slightly, and he felt her starting to panic. He didn't want to scare her, but he wasn't sure how much longer he could stay conscious. He knew he shouldn't fall asleep—he didn't know how much blood he'd lost. But with every passing second, he felt himself shutting down.

He needed to focus. He needed something to focus on that would fill his mind the way he needed right now. He squeezed her hand again, letting her know he was still there.

"Tell me about us," he murmured. "Tell me how you feel about us right now."

She took a deep, shaky breath. She looked out the window for a moment, as though pondering his question, before she responded.

"I thought about us all the time," she murmured to him, looking down at him and even managing a smile. "Even when we were apart, I thought about us. I just couldn't forget you, no matter how much I wanted to, no matter how much easier it would have made my life if I did. If I could have just left you behind, I could have started a new life for myself. I could have moved on…."

She trailed off, then shook her head.

"But that was never going to happen," she confessed. "Even back then, I knew I loved you. Even thinking you'd turned on me. I used to wonder if there was something more to it, because the man I knew…the man I knew would never have done that to me."

She took another breath, closing her eyes for a moment, as though bringing it all back to mind again.

"And I never thought I could live without you forever," she went on. "I always wanted you back in my life. And then, when Ziegler and the others turned on me, there was only one person I could think of to go to for help."

She smiled down at him. "You."

He tightened his grip on her slightly. His vision still wasn't entirely clear, but the sound of her words cut through the confusion around him completely. He couldn't deny how much he loved her, not even if he wanted to. He felt the same way she did, and he was glad to hear her say those words, even if the circumstances were far from perfect.

When he was better again, he would say all of this back to her, make sure she knew how much he cared for her. Just as soon as he could string a sentence together without slurring again.

"And I know I haven't always made it easy for us, you know, since we've been back together again," she continued. "But I think I was just scared. Scared that something was going to pull us apart again. I couldn't have lived with that. It was why I left. I know it doesn't make sense, but it just seemed safer to get out of there before either of us got too attached, especially with Ziegler and the others on our tail."

She shook her head, her face dropping.

"And I wish I could have come back to you without bringing them with me," she whispered, her voice cracking.

He reached up to cup her face, even though his body cried out with every movement. "You didn't bring them," he murmured. "They were always going to come find me. I'm just glad you trusted me enough to help you when you needed it most, even after what happened. I would do anything to protect you. You know that, right?"

"I know that," she replied. "I can see it now."

He smiled, dropping his hand back down to his side with a wince.

A silence hung in the air between them. The only sound was the wheels of the car bumping over the road. And then, he spoke again.

"And what about...our future?" he asked her. "You've covered our past. And our present. What do you think's going to happen now?"

She parted her lips, trying to find the words to express what she wanted to say. Maybe it was unfair of him to ask her so soon after they had taken down the men who'd been chasing her. But he wanted to know—he wanted to be sure she saw the same future for them that he did. Up until an hour or so ago, they hadn't been able to think past the immediate threat. But now? Now, they could do just about anything they wanted.

"I want to join the force again," she replied firmly. "And do everything I can to make sure people like them are weeded out of whatever departments they're infecting right now. I can't stand the thought of more of them out there, and more people who are working with them and don't even know it. If they hadn't tried to pull me into it, I would have just worked with them without knowing. I'm never going to let that happen again."

He could hear the certainty in her voice, and it made him proud. She had come so far since she had been a rookie, but she'd had the same determination and certainty since day one. She had always been ready to take on the world, and now she would. He could tell. And he wanted to be there to support her every step of the way.

"And what about the lodge?" he asked her, his voice weaker.

"What about it?" she replied, looking down at him and brushing another strand of hair away from his face.

"You think you'll stay?"

She smiled slightly, cocking her head at him. "Hmm," she murmured, tapping her finger against her bottom lip. "I don't know about that. Would have to be some pretty good reasons to stay, right?"

"Wheatie?" he suggested, and she laughed.

She leaned down to kiss him again. "I can think of a few other reasons," she murmured against his lips before she pulled back. "And there's plenty of work I can do here. You said Sheriff Willis is a good guy, right? I'm sure he'd be willing to help me with a job."

He gazed up at her, hardly able to keep the smile from his lips. It was exactly what he'd wanted to hear, what he'd needed to hear.

The car pulled to a stop.

"We're here," the driver called to them.

"You're going to be okay," Bailey murmured as she helped him out of the back seat of the car.

"As long as you're here, I will be," he agreed.

But as he stood, he slumped against her, and the last thing he heard was Bailey scream for help as the whole world went black.

Chapter Twenty-Five

Bailey paced back and forth through the hospital waiting room, still bleeding some from her arm. She had too much nervous energy to sit down even though she was exhausted.

As soon as Aaron had passed out in front of the hospital, nurses and doctors had whisked him away on a gurney and straight into surgery to remove the bullet from his torso. She had run alongside him until she wasn't allowed any further, shooing away the nurses who were trying to fuss over her injuries.

"I'm fine," she had insisted. "Go take care of Aaron, please."

The surgeon had come out to tell her that the bullet had been successfully removed from his torso and that if the bullet had entered just a millimeter to the right, he wouldn't have been so lucky.

Lucky.

As it was, Aaron was still unconscious. Recovering from surgery, blood loss, and a gunshot wound just shy of hitting important internal organs. She knew the doctor meant to be encouraging, but right now, things didn't feel so *lucky*.

The doctor had also said that all she could do now was

wait. Wait there in the same room she'd been in since they had arrived, wait for Aaron to wake up, wait to see what his long-term recovery looked like.

She decided she was done waiting.

She marched up to the closest nurses' station and put on her best charming smile even though she knew she must look crazy—bleeding and disheveled—from what she'd been through.

She took a calming breath. "Hi, I need to see my friend. We came in together. He was shot and just got out of surgery, and I need to be with him when he wakes up."

The nurse looked a bit shocked but quickly regained her composure. "Ma'am, you seem to be injured as well. Can we have a doctor look at you?"

"No," Bailey replied forcefully, "I just need to see Aaron Ward."

The nurse smiled patiently. "Okay, I can take you to his room, but maybe you could let someone bandage up that shoulder once you're there."

She nodded in agreement and the nurse led the way down the maze of identical hallways to the room where Aaron was lying, still unconscious, from his surgery.

Just seeing the rise and fall of his chest eased some of the anxiety in her stomach. She let out a relieved breath as she walked across the room to his side.

"I'll send someone in to look at your shoulder and any other injuries," the nurse said before closing the door behind her.

Sure enough, a different nurse came in a few minutes later to clean up, stitch, and bandage her injured shoulder, and look her over for any other injuries. Once that was done, she sat in the chair next to Aaron, holding his hand and waiting for him to wake up.

Her eyes started to get heavy as she listened to the rhythmic beeping of the heart monitor. She decided to climb into the bed next to Aaron and close her eyes, just for a few minutes. She knew she shouldn't—she was filthy, after all—but she just wanted to be close to him right now. She'd rest a few minutes and then she'd wake up before he did and be the first thing he saw when he opened his eyes.

She curled up next to Aaron's uninjured side and dozed off thinking about how thankful she was that they were both alive. And she realized that at that moment, lying next to Aaron, *lucky* was exactly how she felt.

Bailey woke to the feel of someone's fingers running through her hair, and it took her a moment to figure out where she was.

The smell of antiseptic filled her nostrils, and she sat up. Oh God, she remembered now. She had insisted on being let into Aaron's room after his surgery, and had fallen asleep lying in the hospital bed next to him.

He had collapsed just outside of the hospital, and the panic that had run through her veins in that moment was unlike anything she had ever felt before. She blamed herself for getting him involved in this situation and she was furious at the crooked cops who had hurt them both so much, both physically and emotionally.

But, as she opened her eyes, she saw that he was awake and smiling at her. She threw her arms around him and hugged him tight, emotion rising up inside of her.

"You're okay," she gasped.

"Well, I feel like I just got shot." He grunted at the

impact of her attack, but she could hear the smile in his voice. She sprang back, eyes wide.

"Oh, I'm so sorry," she blurted out, realizing she had applied pressure to his fresh wound.

"No, it's okay," he replied. "It feels a lot better than it did when I passed out. Sorry for giving you that scare, by the way."

"Yeah, you should be sorry," she joked, swatting him playfully on the arm as she shook her head. "You scared the hell out of me!"

"My bad." He smiled, and she grinned back.

"How are you feeling?" he asked her, nodding to the bandage on her shoulder. She had wanted the nurses to focus on Aaron instead of her, but she was thankful they had taken care of her wound as well. She'd hardly been paying attention to it, ordering the nurses to focus on him instead, but she was thankful they'd ignored her.

"I'm fine," she replied. "Better than ever, actually."

And even though Aaron was waking up in a hospital bed today, it was the truth. She and Aaron were alive and they would both be okay, though they'd need some time to heal and get back on their feet. But, this time around, they weren't going to have to look over their shoulders the whole time for fear of someone coming after them. Ziegler and his cronies were behind bars, and there was already an ongoing investigation into what they had been up to. They were going to spend a long time in prison for what they had done.

"Have you heard anything about Ziegler and the others?" he asked.

She nodded. "Yeah, I spoke to Willis while you were in surgery and it sounds like they've got plenty to work with just in the van—unregistered weapons, stuff like that."

What she left out was the shovel, rope, and plastic wrappings they had found in there, too. The shovel was no doubt going to be used to dig her grave if they had succeeded in finishing her off. The rest, she didn't want to think about. She'd already be having nightmares for a while to come. She didn't want him knowing about that part, either. It just didn't seem fair to put him through that when he was the one who had taken a bullet.

"And the fire?" he asked.

"There were a few empty gas canisters in the van," she explained. "It seems like way too much of a coincidence for something like that to have happened on the same night they were there on the road to Warrior Peak, so they'll most likely be charged with arson, too."

She paused for a moment before asking quietly, "How bad was the damage to the lodge?"

Nobody had given her a straight answer yet, like they knew she would find a way to blame herself. And of course she did—it was because of her all of this had happened. If she hadn't come to the sanctuary, the guys would never have tracked her down there. In her mind, she was at fault as much as the men who had started the fire.

"It wasn't as bad as I thought it was going to be," he replied neutrally. "There's still plenty of work that needs to be done in the paddocks to get them right again, but it will be summer soon. Things will start growing back quicker than you think."

She smiled at him. That was a relief, and she hoped he was being totally honest with her. Warrior Peak Sanctuary was such a beautiful and peaceful place, she couldn't stand the thought of it being ruined.

"And what about the horses?" she asked. They had been on her mind ever since she had left.

"They're okay," he replied at once. "River and Hannah helped me get them out of the way of the fire. Wheatie was pretty freaked, but I think she'll calm down when she sees you again."

"I think you vastly overestimate my horse-wrangling skills." She laughed, squeezing his hand. She sat up and stretched as much as she could while yawning. She could have slept for a week and not felt rested. After everything she had been through in the last few days, she shouldn't be surprised about that. She hadn't expected to come out alive, but now she was here with the man she loved, and she couldn't imagine anything else that mattered.

"You going to come back to the sanctuary with me?" he asked, and she nodded at once.

"Everything I said last night, I meant it," she promised him. When he had asked her about their future, it hadn't taken her long to realize what she wanted. When it came to him—when it came to them—she had to give it a chance. She wanted to find out what lay ahead for the two of them. They could finally let go of all the stress and fear, and find out how they would be as a normal couple.

Well, after all that had happened, she doubted that the two of them would ever be a normal couple. But they could be a happy one. And that was all she cared about.

"I want to go back to the sanctuary with you," she continued. "And I want to help you in your recovery. You've got some of the best people around you to help with that, and I know Xavier and Lawson want to do everything they can to get you back on your feet."

"Just so I can get to fixing fences again." Aaron chuckled.

Bailey shook her head. "You should give yourself more credit than that," she told him. "They really like you there. I know you've mostly kept to yourself since you got there, but this could be your chance to open up and get to know people and let them get to know you."

Aaron nodded. She could see it made sense to him. He had been avoiding putting down roots because he had been scared of his past catching up to him, but he didn't need to fear that any longer. He could put that all aside now, and just let himself be the person he wanted to be.

"You're right," he murmured, skimming his thumb over her knuckles. "I've already done a little of that, but I think it'll be easier with you around."

"That's not the only reason I'm staying," she promised him softly. "I... I really want to try and make things work between us, Aaron. God knows what we've got is complicated, but I want to give it a try. When I'm with you, I feel... I feel something I've never felt before. I want to see where that takes us."

"I don't think it's complicated at all." He smiled. "I think it's completely straightforward. I'm in love with you, and I want to spend every day of the rest of my life proving to you just how much I mean that."

"Oh, Aaron," she breathed, and she leaned over to kiss his lips. She was just so overwhelmed with emotion, she hardly knew where to start in sorting through it. But the one at the top of her list, the one that most stood out to her, was sheer and utter gratitude. Gratitude that despite everything that had happened, the path to their future finally seemed clear.

"I love you, Aaron," she murmured to him. She would never get tired of saying those words to him, she was sure of it. When she looked at him, she just wanted to tell him over and over again.

"I love you too, Bailey," he replied.

She closed her eyes for a moment, letting the sweetness of this moment linger. She couldn't wait to get back to Warrior Peak with him, so the two of them could settle into their new life together—whatever that happened to look like. As long as they were together, she didn't care at all. Whatever she did next, as long as it was with him by her side, she would be happy.

Chapter Twenty-Six

"You want to go feed Wheatie?" Aaron asked Bailey, as she grabbed an apple from the breakfast table. She always picked up a piece of fruit when she wanted to see her favorite horse. She never felt like she could visit the mare without some kind of treat, and the horse was never going to turn her down.

"You read my mind," she replied, looping her free hand into his arm. "I'm not keeping you from anything?"

"I'm all good," he replied, slipping an arm around her waist. "I've got the day off. Got physical therapy with Carter."

"Ah, of course," she said. "How's it going?"

"I really don't think I need to be going anymore," he grumbled slightly. "I'm totally better. It's been more than six months since I got shot."

"Yes, well, better to be safe than sorry, right?" she told him.

He grinned at her. "I know better than to argue with you," he replied.

She laughed. "Damn right you do," she agreed, tossing up the apple and catching it in her hand again as they stepped out of the door. She'd actually finished her own physical therapy sessions not long ago and got a clean bill of health. Between the knife wound in her leg and then her shoulder, she'd had some work to do of her own to heal up properly.

The sun blazed down, a late fall day alive with the gold and red of the trees. More than half a year after the attack on Warrior Peak by Ziegler and his men, things were finally starting to get back to normal, and he couldn't have been happier.

In fact, the day before he had spent most of the afternoon planting rows of flowers and grass in and around the paddock. Bailey had offered to help him, but he knew she had an appointment with Willis to talk over some more of the evidence that had come to light, and he didn't want to keep her from that. Besides, it was a chance for him to get back to reality, a chance for him to forget about all the limitations that had been on him as he had been recovering from getting shot.

Of course, they hadn't felt like limitations with Bailey around. She had been there to help him out every step of the way, literally. He had struggled with walking for the first couple of weeks, the pain sometimes getting to be too much for him, and she would patiently take him over to the cafeteria for breakfast without a word of complaint. After that, she helped with his physical therapy on the side, learning the best exercises for him to do and making sure he always got them done. She liked to crack the whip, but he was thankful for that. It kept him on track. He had finally been allowed to get back to doing some work the month before, though Xavier and Lawson had both tried to talk him out of it, and they wouldn't let him do everything he was doing before he got shot.

"You don't need to push yourself," Xavier had tried

to warn him. "You don't want to do too much and have a setback with your recovery. The work will still be there when you're ready."

"At this point, I think I'm putting it back more by not getting out there and doing something," he had protested. "I need to feel like I'm doing something useful. You guys get that, right?"

"You're resting," Lawson had told him. "Sometimes, that's the most useful thing you can do."

"Besides, it's not like you haven't been busy helping out with the case," Xavier had pointed out—a fair thing to bring up.

Aaron and Bailey had been working with Willis and a few other cops across the state with the case against Ziegler and his crew. Not that it was actually going to court. At the moment, it looked like they would each be taking a plea deal. It wasn't ideal, and Aaron would have preferred to see them made an example of, but he got it. The information they handed over might have been enough to get to the bottom of a few cold cases, and those victims deserved justice.

And at the end of the day, he didn't care how they went away, as long as they were out of his life, and Bailey's life, for good. It had taken a long time for Bailey to recover emotionally from what she had been through, and even now, he sometimes found her awake after a nightmare. But, these days, he could usually coax her back to bed and hold her until she fell asleep.

She'd even recently agreed to meet with Sarah, the counselor at the sanctuary. He had finally shared with her about how he came to be at Warrior Peak all those years ago. How messed up his head was, paranoid of being tracked down or worse, and how Sarah had helped him overcome some of the worst of the nightmares. After listening to Aaron voice the details so similar to her own, she'd decided it might be good for her, too. Just to round out her healing, and Aaron couldn't have been more proud of her for that.

Bailey had settled in at Warrior Peak amazingly well, and was working with Willis down in Blue Ridge to help put the pieces of the case together. She had even dropped in a few mentions about working with him long-term, and Aaron truly hoped she would. Blue Ridge wasn't all that different from Kings Mountain, and it would give her a fresh place to start over.

They arrived at the paddock, where Wheatie was already working her way through some of the flowers Aaron had planted there the day before. He had done everything he could to help erase the damage caused by the fire.

"Hey, you!" he called to the horse.

Wheatie lifted her head long enough to snort in their direction, and then went right back to eating the flowers.

He sighed and shook his head.

"I told you this would happen," Bailey teased him. She had—she'd reminded him of how Wheatie had gone through the flowers before, and suggested putting up some new fences before he started work on replanting, but he hadn't listened.

"This is supposed to be where the plants are regrowing," he reminded Wheatie as he reached the fence. "You're not going to let that happen as long as you keep eating them."

"Hey, leave her alone," Bailey protested, reaching over

the fence to pat Wheatie on the nose. She and Wheatie had such an amazing bond. Wheatie lifted her head to stop eating for a moment to greet her friend.

"Here, I brought you an apple," she continued, offering the fruit in her hand. Wheatie carefully wrapped her lips around it and then snapped it up, making Bailey laugh.

"And now you've just rewarded her for eating my plants," Aaron pointed out.

Bailey shrugged. "You can't blame a horse for horsing," she replied. "She deserves it. She worked very hard supervising you, you know."

"I should have known you would take her side in an argument over mine," he replied, but he couldn't help but grin. This side of her, this softer side, was one he was falling more in love with every day.

"Yeah, I always will, sorry," she replied, tossing her hair over one shoulder and flashing him a playful grin. "Come on—let's take a look at the flowers, and see if there might be anything to salvage, huh?"

She slipped her hand into his and guided him toward the other side of the paddock. Thankfully, Wheatie had done less damage over there, and it looked like there would be enough for them to work with.

"Well, I guess it's something," he muttered, and she leaned into him.

"It's going to be overflowing with green again soon enough," she promised him. "You've done a great job here. And I know it's not going to be long until you start to reap the rewards."

"Oh, I think I've already got plenty of those," he murmured, and she smiled as he leaned his head down to hers to give her a kiss. He meant it—she was a greater reward than anything he could ever have asked for. Sometimes, their closeness didn't even feel like it could be real to him, but it was. It was as real as the sun beaming down on them from the sky above, and just as warm.

They headed back to the main building to help with preparing dinner. It was a ritual they had gotten into doing a few times a week, spending some time together and helping Cade and the others make some delicious food. One of the new arrivals had even started a vegetable garden, giving them fresh produce to use. It was these quiet, domestic times they spent together that Aaron loved the most. It made him imagine what living with her in a real house would look like. He was in no rush to leave the sanctuary, not for a long time, but getting to picture her in a home of their own made him smile.

They served up dinner for everyone, and the core group crowded around the center table. Xavier, Lawson, and Hannah on one side, Cade and River on the other, along with Bailey and Aaron.

"This looks great," Hannah remarked as she went to serve herself up a generous helping.

"Hey, leave some for the rest of us," Lawson teased, nudging her, and she raised her eyebrows at him pointedly.

"First come, first served!" she retorted, and everyone laughed.

While they were all eating Lawson asked, "You had a meeting with Willis yesterday, didn't you, Bailey?"

"Yeah, I did." She nodded.

"How did it go?" Xavier asked. "How's the case coming along? Anything they need us to give them a hand with?"

"I think they're okay for the time being," she replied, smiling down at her plate. "But, uh, there was something we got to talking about. I wanted to tell everyone when we were all together."

Aaron's heart leaped in his chest, and he reached over to squeeze her hand beneath the table. She shot him a slightly nervous look, biting her lip, but he nodded at her to go on. He could tell everyone was on pins and needles, waiting for her to share her news.

"I asked him if there were any positions open in the Blue Ridge police force, and he said yes," she explained. River drew in a sharp breath, and Hannah clapped her hands together.

Aaron could hardly believe it. He thought she would have come to him first about this, but from the look on her face, he could tell she wanted to be sure before she told him anything. She never liked to get his hopes up without good reason, and this was about the best one he could imagine.

"That's amazing!" Hannah exclaimed, jumping to her feet and rushing around the table to give her a hug. Bailey smiled and hugged her back; the two women had become close in her time here. They, along with River, could often be found walking in the forest together.

"Yeah, I know it's not exactly what I pictured for my career," she continued, once Hannah had released her. "But I can work really closely with him on the case against Ziegler and the others, and maybe work my way up to a bigger agency from there."

"But that means you're going to be staying for now, right?" Hannah asked enthusiastically.

Bailey nodded. "Yeah, it does."

"Then this meal is a celebration!" Hannah exclaimed, grabbing her glass and lifting it up. "To Bailey. And her first year at Warrior Peak!"

"First of many, I hope," River added, and Bailey flushed excitedly. She glanced over to Aaron, and Aaron could do nothing more than smile back at her.

"To Bailey," Lawson announced, and everyone echoed him, their words overlapping as their glasses tapped together.

"Thank you," Bailey replied, lowering her head in gratitude. "It means so much to me that you're all happy I'm staying."

"Of course we are!" Hannah replied, but Aaron knew one thing for sure. As much as everyone here was happy she was sticking around—nobody was more excited about what this meant than him.

He leaned over and brushed his lips against her ear. "I love you. And I'm so proud of you."

Chapter Twenty-Seven

Bailey woke up slowly to the feel of Aaron rubbing her back lightly. She rolled toward him with a sleepy smile on her face.

"Good morning, beautiful," he said softly, giving her a quick kiss.

She beamed. "Good morning, handsome."

No matter how many times she woke up next to him, she was always so happy that he was the first thing she saw when she opened her eyes every morning. She still felt giddy when he kissed her, and got butterflies just from looking at him. She didn't think she would ever get over how thankful she was that they had found each other again.

"It's your first official day of work today at the Blue Ridge Police Department. How are you feeling about it?"

That was one thing she loved about Aaron—he was always so thoughtful and he cared about her feelings. "I'm excited," she replied. "A little anxious, too, if I'm being honest. The last first day I had at a police department didn't go so well." She shrugged a shoulder.

He tucked a strand of hair behind her ear. "That's true, but just remember that Blue Ridge isn't Kings Mountain, and there are more good cops out there than ones like what we dealt with from Kings Mountain."

She sighed. "I know you're right. I'm excited to be part of the department here. Willis has been such a big help with our case."

"You have a lot to offer the BRPD. I've always known you were a good cop, even before I fell in love with you," Aaron said.

Bailey smiled. "Right back at you, Ward."

Aaron laughed. "Want to make some breakfast together before you have to get ready to go?"

She sat up and swung her legs off the side of the bed. "Yes, that sounds great."

They made their way into the tiny kitchen of the cabin where they lived. Even though it was a small, cramped space, it was sentimental to Bailey because it was their first place together. She knew that someday they would need to find another bigger place, but for now, she was happy right where they were.

They worked together like a well-oiled machine. Bailey brewed the coffee and set the table while Aaron scrambled eggs and made some toast. Then they sat down to eat breakfast together, like they did almost every day. They chatted comfortably about the sanctuary, their friends, and Aaron's plans for the day while Bailey was at work.

After they cleaned up their dishes, Bailey took a shower and got dressed for work. She looked at herself in the full-length mirror—it almost felt strange to be wearing a uniform again after everything that had happened. It felt good, though. Being a police officer was what she was meant to do. She'd never been more sure of that.

She walked out of the bedroom and into the small living room where Aaron was, and did a flirty little spin like she was a supermodel at the end of a runway. "What do you think?"

Aaron whistled. "Hottest new cop I've ever seen in Blue Ridge," he said, linking his arms around her waist.

She swatted his chest playfully. "You probably say that to all the new cops."

He tipped his head back and laughed. "I can assure you, I definitely do not."

She went up on her toes and kissed him. "I love you. I'll see you tonight."

"I love you, too. You're going to kill it today, and I can't wait to hear about it when you get back."

Bailey smiled as she walked out the front door of the cabin to her truck. She couldn't wait to see what the day had in store for her.

BAILEY DROVE DOWN the mountain toward the town of Blue Ridge, thinking about the accident she'd had on that very road just a few months earlier. Although it was a scary, horrible, painful situation, ultimately it was what had allowed them to arrest Ziegler and his band of crooked cops, and get justice for the people who had suffered because of them.

She pulled into the parking lot of the small-town police department and took a deep breath, gathering her courage. She knew Willis and had met many of the other officers while working the case to put the corrupt cops behind bars. It was also part of living in a small town—almost everyone knew each other in some capacity, even if the only interaction they had was a friendly wave when their paths crossed at a local store.

She realized that she enjoyed small-town life more than she thought she would. When she thought back to her time working behind a desk in a small beach town and how much she wanted to get back to Kings Mountain, she couldn't believe how her life, and desires, had changed. She didn't need fast-paced and dangerous. She was perfectly content to make sure that Blue Ridge stayed the safe and quiet little town it was. Of course, Aaron being in the safe and quiet little town had a lot to do with her change of heart as well.

With one last calming breath, she stepped out of her truck and walked toward the front doors of the police station. Once inside, she walked up to the front desk, where a pleasant-looking older woman sat.

"Hi, I'm—" she started.

"Bailey!" the woman exclaimed, her face lighting up with a smile. "I know who you are, honey. Sheriff Willis is waiting for you in his office. Do you want me to show you the way?"

Bailey couldn't help but smile back at the kind woman. "You don't have to do that. I know the way."

The woman nodded. "Okay, dear, but let me know if you need anything. My name is Evelyn." She leaned in conspiratorially. "I keep these officers here in line like they're my own children. You be sure to let me know if anyone gives you any problems."

Bailey's smile widened. "Thank you, Evelyn. I'll be sure to let you know."

"See that you do," Evelyn replied, waving her off toward the sheriff's office.

Bailey was still smiling from her interaction with Evelyn as she walked down to Willis's office, finding the door open. He was on the phone but motioned for her to come in and have a seat in one of the chairs in front of his desk. She looked around the room while he finished his phone call. On the walls were awards and certificates, and on his desk and credenza behind it were pictures of his wife, kids, and grandkids. She smiled at one particular picture of a little boy, face smudged with mud, holding up a tiny fish and grinning broadly like it was his prized possession.

Sheriff Willis said his goodbyes to the person he was talking to and hung up the phone. "Sorry to be on the phone when you first arrive, Bailey."

"No apology necessary, sir, I know you're a busy man," she replied.

Willis nodded his thanks. "I take it you met Evelyn out at the front desk?"

"Yes," she confirmed. "She seems very nice."

"Oh, she is," he replied. "Just don't get on her bad side. One time I tracked mud through the lobby after I had been walking through the woods in the rain for a case. She was so mad that I had to bring her that fancy coffee she likes every morning for a week before she would forgive me."

Bailey chuckled. "No to mud, yes to coffee. Noted."

"I think you're going to fit in here just fine," he said with a smile. "Do you want to go meet the others before I show you the ropes and give you the whole introductory spiel?"

Her stomach flipped but she nodded confidently. "Yes, that sounds great."

She followed behind Sheriff Willis as he led her out to the bullpen where the officers' desks were.

"Everyone, this is Bailey," Sheriff Willis said over the din of the busy environment. "Bailey, this is everyone." He swept an arm around the room.

Bailey smiled and waved awkwardly. "Uh, hi, everyone."

"You'll have a chance to learn everyone's names and get to know them personally soon," Sheriff Willis promised.

Throughout the day, almost every single person found Bailey to talk to her and kindly welcome her to the department. Some of them asked questions about how Aaron was doing or how things were going with the rebuilding of the parts of the sanctuary that were damaged in the fire. She realized that she had no reason to be worried about these people being like the guys she had worked with in Kings Mountain. Aaron had been right—they were good cops and good people. She was excited to be a part of this group of officers.

By the end of the day she was tired but happy. Some of the officers invited her to grab a beer at the local bar after their shift, but she declined, promising to join them next time. She didn't say no because she was worried about a repeat of what had happened at the bar in Kings Mountain, but because all she wanted to do was get home to Aaron and tell him about her day.

She got in her truck and drove back toward Warrior Peak. She waved at Hannah and River, who were taking a walk, as she drove by but didn't stop to talk. She would give them all the details about her first day on the job tomorrow. Right now, the only person she wanted to talk to was Aaron.

When she pulled up in front of their cabin, she paused for a moment, taking in its charm. Sure, it was small and rustic and the hot water didn't always work, but if home was truly where the heart was, then this was definitely home. At the end of a long day, that's all she could ask for.

She got out of her truck and walked into the cabin to find Aaron cooking dinner. He turned and smiled when she came in.

"Hello, officer," he said with mischief in his eyes. "I promise I'm not doing anything illegal."

She tried to look stern, playing along. "I sure hope not, or else I might have to handcuff you."

He waggled his eyebrows. "Is that so?"

She nodded solemnly. "Yes, and I was given my department-issued cuffs today, so you better watch it, buddy."

He laughed. "Let's save that for later. First, let's eat and you can tell me all about your day."

"That sounds like a good plan," she said. "I'm starving and whatever you're making smells delicious."

They sat down and ate together, and she told him all about her day. The people she'd met, how kind they'd been, and how much she looked forward to working for the department. Aaron listened and asked a few questions, then told her about his day. He'd had some physical therapy and then worked on some small projects that he had convinced Lawson and Xavier to let him do.

"Sounds like we both had a pretty productive day," Aaron said.

Bailey nodded in agreement. "Are you ready to do it all over again tomorrow?"

"I guess so," Aaron replied. "But first, I have some other plans for us tonight."

"Do you?" she said coyly, standing up from the table.

He stood, too, and grabbed her around her hips, lifting her off the ground. "I sure do. Let me show you."

She wrapped her legs around his waist as he walked them into the bedroom, and couldn't remember a time she was so content in all areas of her life.

She was finally where she was meant to be.

Chapter Twenty-Eight

Aaron looked around the cabin that he and Bailey shared and sighed. Things were quiet now that she worked and wasn't around all day. He was so incredibly proud of her, but he missed her when she was gone. He had gotten used to slow mornings, midday walks to visit Wheatie and give her treats, afternoon coffee on the tiny back porch of their cabin, and cooking dinner together every night.

They could still do those things sometimes, just not every day like they had been. It didn't help that he wasn't fully back to work, building and doing other physical jobs around the lodge grounds. He could admit that he was a little envious of Bailey being able to put that uniform on each morning and go to work helping people. While he didn't want to be a police officer anymore, he did want to do something that mattered.

He felt like what he did at the sanctuary mattered. Now, if he could just convince Lawson and Xavier that he was healed up enough to go fully back to his job. He'd been consistent with his physical therapy and going to all of his doctor's appointments. He felt strong and capable of returning to work. He decided he was going to go talk to Lawson and Xavier about it right then and there.

He made his way to the main building, stopping to

pet Wheatie and give her an apple. Even though Wheatie seemed happy to see him, she looked past him as if she was searching for Bailey. When she didn't see her, she turned doleful eyes back to Aaron.

"I know you miss her, girl," he said softly to the horse, stroking her silky head. "I do, too, but she'll be back this evening and I know she'll want to come out here to see you."

Wheatie nudged him gently with her nose and snorted like she understood what he was saying. With one more pat, he left Wheatie in the paddock and continued toward the lodge. He was a little bit nervous about this conversation with Xavier and Lawson, because not only did he want to talk about fully returning to work, but he also had something else important that he wanted to ask them.

When he stepped through the doors of the lodge building, he saw Hannah.

He waved at her. "Hey, Hannah, have you seen Lawson and Xavier? I was hoping to have a meeting with both of them."

Hannah's brows shot up. "Yeah, I think they're both in Lawson's office. Is everything okay?"

"Yep. Everything is great," he replied reassuringly.

Something like relief passed over her face. He knew she worried about everyone after the fire and the other things that had happened that night.

"How is Bailey liking her new job at the police department?" she asked. "I feel like I haven't had much of a chance to talk to her about it because she's been so busy."

"She's really loving it," he said with pride in his voice.

"I'm so glad to hear that." Hannah smiled. "Hopefully, I'll catch up with her soon. But for now, I'm going to let you go track down the guys, and I need to head to town for some supplies."

They said their goodbyes and Aaron continued down the hallway toward the offices. When he reached the outside of Lawson's office, he knocked twice.

"Come in," Lawson called.

Aaron opened the door and poked his head in, where he saw both Lawson and Xavier, just as Hannah had predicted. "Hey guys, I was hoping to have a conversation with you. Do you have a few minutes?"

Xavier and Lawson exchanged glances before looking back at him. "Sure," Xavier said, gesturing to a chair next to him. "What's on your mind, Aaron?"

Aaron took a seat and a fortifying breath before jumping in. "I'm ready to start working again."

Lawson looked confused. "You have been working."

"No." Aaron shook his head. "I mean, like my real work. I want to get back to building and all of the things I was doing before my injury and surgery. Not the easy little odd jobs you've been creating to make me feel useful."

"Aaron," Xavier started. "You were shot only a few months ago. We just want you to have a chance to heal up before you're back to climbing ladders and doing all of the other things you do."

Aaron made eye contact with each of them. "I am healed up. My doctor cleared me and he said I can go back to my life—and work—as usual."

The men smiled genuinely. "That's great news, Aaron," Xavier said. "Just promise to let one of us know if something is too much or if you start to feel like you need to take a step back again."

"I will," Aaron promised, and excitement bloomed in his chest.

"Was there anything else you wanted to talk to us about?" Lawson asked.

"Actually, yes, there is..." Aaron trailed off, trying to decide how he was going to bring up this next topic he wanted to talk to them about. "It's about Bailey and me."

For the next hour, Aaron, Lawson, and Xavier talked through logistics, asked questions, and Aaron showed and explained the plans he had.

"Bailey doesn't know any of this yet, though," he warned. "I would appreciate it if you could keep this between us for the time being."

Lawson and Xavier agreed.

By the time Aaron left Lawson's office, he was so excited and relieved. And for the first time in a long time, he was looking toward the future, instead of dwelling on the past. He knew exactly who to thank for that.

With Bailey by his side, he knew there was nothing they couldn't accomplish together.

Forever.

Epilogue

Bailey edged the car to a halt at the edge of the path, letting out a long sigh as she pulled her hair from her ponytail and shook it loose. No matter how long the day, no matter how hard the case, she was always glad to come back to this place. It was home to her. But more importantly, it was home to Aaron, and she couldn't wait to see him.

She climbed out of the front seat and locked up the car, then tucked her keys into her pocket. She'd been given her own cruiser a couple of months ago, and she was still proud to drive it. A reminder of how far she had come, and how well she had done in earning Willis's trust.

It had been nearly a year since she'd arrived at Warrior Peak Sanctuary, and the difference between her then and her now was almost staggering. When she'd gotten here, she'd been a scared little girl, on the run for her life. Now, she was a self-assured woman who had a thriving career and a reputation for bringing down the shadiest cops in the business.

The relief of knowing that the men who had tormented her and Aaron were behind bars was immense to her, even more than she thought it would be. They had each been put away on plea deals, and a handful of cold cases had already been solved based on evidence they had obscured or destroyed, with a few more well on their way to the same end. She had been working with the victims directly, doing what she could to restore their faith in the police after what they had been through. She could only imagine how hard it had been for them, and she was able to relate to them based on her own experiences with Ziegler and his gang.

She made her way up the path to the cabin where she and Aaron had been staying for the past year. It was small, but it wasn't like they needed much space from each other anyway. He had been teasing her since they had first moved in together that he had been keeping her flexible through his physical therapy, and she supposed with their bedroom antics, he was kind of right. A flicker of a smile passed over her lips as she looped the final corner to their cabin.

Aaron was sitting out on the back porch, in the chair he'd grabbed from a dump and started to fix up in his own time. It was something he had really gotten into over the last few months, restoring old furniture. Most of it, he donated to local charities, but some pieces they had kept for their place. It was starting to feel like a real home, and she found herself craving something even more like that.

He looked up from his lap when he saw her coming over. It still felt a little strange to be in uniform and him not, but when he looked at her with such appreciation in his eyes, nothing else mattered. She made her way up the steps to the porch, and looked down at what he was working on. Spread across his lap was a blueprint, covered in small pencil strokes here and there.

"What's this you're working on?" she asked, and he lifted the blueprint from his lap and patted his leg, indicating for her to come take a seat.

"Just working on a building design," he said.

She draped her arms around his shoulders. "Talk me through it."

"Well, this is going to be the entryway," he explained, tracing his finger along the paper. "And this is going to be the living room. Through here, the main bedroom, and down this hallway, a nice kitchen with a big window looking out over the mountains…"

"Wow, this place looks amazing," she murmured. "What is it for? Is the sanctuary opening up new places to stay, or something?"

He glanced up at her, a smile on his face, and shook his head. "Nope, it's not for Warrior Peak," he replied.

She furrowed her brow, confused. "Then who is it for?"

"It's for us," he replied simply, and her eyes widened as she looked down at the page.

"You're designing this for us?" she whispered in shock. She had seen him working on these pages a few times, but she had always figured it was something for the sanctuary she would find out about eventually.

But a home? For them? It made her head spin with the possibilities.

"Yeah, I want to give you a real home," he replied. "A place we can live. A place with room to start a family, if that's what you want."

"Oh, Aaron." She sighed and leaned down to kiss him. She couldn't think of a damn thing in the world more romantic than what he had just said to her.

"I would love that," she added, brushing her nose against his. "And where exactly is this palace going to be?"

"I already spoke to Xavier and Lawson," he replied. "To see if they'd be willing to give up a little bit of the sanctuary grounds for us."

She gasped. "And what did they say?"

"They said yes," he replied with a grin.

She squealed and wrapped her arms around him even tighter, pushing her head into his shoulder. "That's the most amazing news," she breathed. So she could stay here with Aaron, continue her work with Willis, and they could start putting down real roots. Just like the grass that had regrown to cover the paddock and the flowers around it, they could settle here and find a place to bloom. A family? He had said something about a family, and her heart fluttered at the thought.

"I love you so much, Aaron," she told him, and he ran his hand along her back, a small, simple gesture that made her whole body tingle.

"I love you, too, Bailey," he murmured back.

For a moment, they just sat in the silence. The birds were chirping in the trees around them, the same songs they had been singing when she had first arrived, but her future looked a whole lot brighter than it had back then.

And she could hardly wait to see what else was in store for her.

* * * * *

Get up to 4 Free Books!

We'll send you 2 free books from each series you try PLUS a free Mystery Gift.

FREE Value Over **$25**

Both the **Harlequin Intrigue®** and **Harlequin® Romantic Suspense** series feature compelling novels filled with heart-racing action-packed romance that will keep you on the edge of your seat.

YES! Please send me 2 FREE novels from the Harlequin Intrigue or Harlequin Romantic Suspense series and my FREE gift (gift is worth about $10 retail). After receiving them, if I don't wish to receive any more books, I can return the shipping statement marked "cancel." If I don't cancel, I will receive 6 brand-new Harlequin Intrigue Larger-Print books every month and be billed just $7.19 each in the U.S. or $7.99 each in Canada, or 4 brand-new Harlequin Romantic Suspense books every month and be billed just $6.39 each in the U.S. or $7.19 each in Canada, a savings of 20% off the cover price. It's quite a bargain! Shipping and handling is just 50¢ per book in the U.S. and $1.25 per book in Canada.* I understand that accepting the 2 free books and gift places me under no obligation to buy anything. I can always return a shipment and cancel at any time by calling the number below. The free books and gift are mine to keep no matter what I decide.

Choose one:
- ☐ **Harlequin Intrigue Larger-Print** (199/399 BPA G36Y)
- ☐ **Harlequin Romantic Suspense** (240/340 BPA G36Y)
- ☐ **Or Try Both!** (199/399 & 240/340 BPA G36Z)

Name (please print)

Address / Apt. #

City / State/Province / Zip/Postal Code

Email: Please check this box ☐ if you would like to receive newsletters and promotional emails from Harlequin Enterprises ULC and its affiliates. You can unsubscribe anytime.

Mail to the Harlequin Reader Service:
IN U.S.A.: P.O. Box 1341, Buffalo, NY 14240-8531
IN CANADA: P.O. Box 603, Fort Erie, Ontario L2A 5X3

Want to explore our other series or interested in ebooks? Visit www.ReaderService.com or call 1-800-873-8635.

---

*Terms and prices subject to change without notice. Prices do not include sales taxes, which will be charged (if applicable) based on your state or country of residence. Canadian residents will be charged applicable taxes. Offer not valid in Quebec. This offer is limited to one order per household. Books received may not be as shown. Not valid for current subscribers to the Harlequin Intrigue or Harlequin Romantic Suspense series. All orders subject to approval. Credit or debit balances in a customer's account(s) may be offset by any other outstanding balance owed by or to the customer. Please allow 4 to 6 weeks for delivery. Offer available while quantities last.

Your Privacy—Your information is being collected by Harlequin Enterprises ULC, operating as Harlequin Reader Service. For a complete summary of the information we collect, how we use this information and to whom it is disclosed, please visit our privacy notice located at https://corporate.harlequin.com/privacy-notice. Notice to California Residents – Under California law, you have specific rights to control and access your data. For more information on these rights and how to exercise them, visit https://corporate.harlequin.com/california-privacy. For additional information for residents of other U.S. states that provide their residents with certain rights with respect to personal data, visit https://corporate.harlequin.com/other-state-residents-privacy-rights/.